CLAIMING HIS

FATE

FERAL BREED MOTORCYCLE CLUB
BOOK ONE

ELLIS LEIGH

Kinship Press

Claiming His Fate
Copyright ©2014 by Ellis Leigh
All rights reserved

Second Edition
ISBN: 9780-9862371-0-2

Kinship Press
P.O. Box 221
Prospect heights, IL 60070

Dedicated to all those who came before me on this journey, and the ones working their way down the paths I have tread.

Best of luck to you all!

ONE

Rebel

THE RUMBLE OF SOLID American craftsmanship roared through the empty streets. Already, the sparkly light of a late-spring dawn brightened the tops of the taller buildings in the Detroit skyline. Modern glass and steel structures mixed with art deco showstoppers popular too many decades ago to count. Structures that blocked the light from hitting the ground, leaving the street level in a gloomy sort of darkness.

The darkness grew when I drove past the old train station. The grand dame stood tall and still proud, though dirty and neglected in her old age. Nearly forgotten. A dishonorable thing to do to such an amazing example of Beaux-Arts architecture. The massive structure blocked what little light there was, giving the shadows more ground to cover. Letting them play a little farther out from her walls. And still, I rolled on.

The world had changed so much in the years since I'd been brought into this life. Too much, I often thought. Two hundred years of fighting to survive as a wolf shifter in a world built for humans had left me jaded. Hardened in a way that would have surprised my younger self. Of course, that man had been fully human and ready to fight for every offense he saw. I'd grown older, learned the ways of my wolfy brethren, and no longer jumped into every battle. But when I did, I made sure I won.

As I passed the abandoned train station, I left the darkness behind once more. The sun blared in the eastern sky, still low but lighting my path with its golden rays. Lighting the way to my home.

The residents of Corktown were already stirring as I turned onto my street. Factory workers heading off for a day of labor, teachers and students anxious for the school year to end walking toward their house of education. And my guys, the wolf shifters hidden among the humans in the old, predominantly Irish neighborhood, gearing up for a five-hour ride across the state.

My home, my family, my life…all encompassed in one dilapidated old building in an urban city on cultural life support. My Feral Breed Motorcycle Club denhouse.

Gates, Sergeant-at-Arms of the house, stood at the garage entrance, glaring out at the world as I drove through the bay doors. Motorcycles of all shapes and sizes ate up the floor space of the room, protected from the elements and the seedier side of life in the city behind our walls and security systems. No one touched one of our rides.

"Boss." Gates nodded, waiting as I took off my helmet and dismounted the bike.

"Updates?"

"We leave in ten. I'll act as Road Captain so Klutch can stay and run the den."

"Good. I want both houses monitored and protected while we attend the meetings."

"Taken care of. The guys from the Kalamazoo house arrived about an hour ago."

I led the way into the actual club area of the building, heading down the long hallway at the back to my office door. "Perfect. I'll grab my bag, say a few words, and we'll bolt."

"Understood." The shifter stalked toward the bar area of the club, moving with the confidence of a wild animal that knows it's at the top of the food pyramid. Gates may have been twice as old as I was, but he'd accepted my dominance as the leader of the club with grace. More than some of the guys I'd cut from the roster since I'd assumed the power position. Even in the shifter world, prejudices ran deep, especially when an Anbizen shifter took the lead. One not born into their wolf-shifter status but turned. A half-breed of sorts.

The main area of the denhouse was in its normal state of chaotic control. Men of varying ages and forms filled the space, talking loudly and drinking whatever their preferred beverage happened to be. Even at such an early hour, the bartender was being kept busy. Not at all surprising with our group. Two wolves stalked through the room, weaving between the legs of their den brothers. Their gray fur and dark eyes stood out among the denim and black leather crowd, but they were accepted without pause, just as they would have been in their human form. Also not at all surprising.

"Gentlemen." I raised a hand to indicate a need for quiet, giving my guys time to settle down and focus. Twenty heads turned in my direction, twenty sets of eyes on me. I was the leader of this group, the Alpha of our non-pack, and they all knew it.

"It's time for my road crew to leave. Kalamazoo team, thank you for coming to keep this den guarded while we're in Chicago. Your loyalty to the Eastern Great Lakes Feral Breed is appreciated and will be rewarded. Local guys—" I smirked, knowing the reaction I'd get from my next statement "—make sure our friends here have a good time. They don't have the same sort of nightlife out there in the sticks as we do around here."

The good-natured growls and backslaps broke the silence

of the crowd. I caught the eyes of each of the guys I'd selected to accompany me to Chicago for the quarterly meeting of our national organization. They moved without instruction, coming to stand behind me. A wall of wolf shifter ready to ride.

"Gentlemen, we are the men of the Feral Breed. The protectors of wolf shifters and keepers of the secret of our kind. Proud defenders of our leader and our brothers. Even when not together, we are a unit. A family. And I'm proud as fuck to lead you all."

The room exploded in hoots and growls, the noise making me grin.

"Yo, boss man." The leader of the Kalamazoo den stepped forward, a sarcastic sort of smirk on his face. "Any recommendations for a local honey hole for the ladies?"

Gates chuckled from my left. "With your ugly mug, Crash, I'm pretty sure your only shot is with the local pros."

"No pros in the denhouse," I yelled, regaining the attention of the crowd. "No drugs, no humans unescorted, and no women anywhere except this bar space and the living quarters upstairs. Keep it professional, guys. We have a job to do and need our facilities to do it. If anyone has to interact with the humans of the neighborhood, there's a stash of The Draught that Klutch has access to. If anyone lets an outsider into our den, it's his responsibility to make sure that guest doesn't see what they shouldn't. And for fuck's sake"—I glared at one of my hangers-on, the one my message needed to be directed to— "do not let the women around the bikes unattended."

A couple of guys smacked their heavy hands against the hanger-on's back, giving him a good-natured reminder of the time he tried to impress a woman by taking her into the garage. She'd charmed him into letting her drive one of the bikes of another den member, promptly laying it down when she lost control on the street right outside.

There was a reason the man was just a hanger-on when he'd once been a prospect. Mistakes like that needed to be punished, and a loss in rank was a fitting punishment. Most den leaders would have kicked his ass out.

The guy looked pissed but contrite, as he should have. "Understood, boss. No women in the back. Ever. Especially not on any of the bikes."

"That's right, not-Pup," Gates called as we headed for the garage. "Bitches don't ride."

We mounted up and grouped near the door, the thunder of five bikes and a war wagon running nearly making the walls shake.

"Ready?" I yelled. My guys all nodded or gave a thumbs-up, indicating we were good to go. With a rev of my Victory's engine and a growl to match the motor humming between my legs, I kicked off. Heading for the highway.

Heading for the quarterly meeting of the Feral Breed Motorcycle Club.

TWO

Charlotte

THE CLOCK TICKING IN the corner seemed to boom, giving me a headache as I reached for any thread of getting out of the mess I was in.

"Miss Andrews?" The chief financial officer of the Pendleton Center for the Blind raised his eyebrows at me, seeming irritated with my delay.

"Yes, sir?"

"When can we expect payment for the remainder of your brother's tuition?"

If my mouth could have gotten any drier, a fire would have started from how hard I ground my teeth. Four years. For four damned years, I'd scrimped and saved and worked my ass off to keep my brother at the school his doctors and social workers had said was the best. And it was all going to end if I didn't figure out a way to hustle harder.

"Well, you see, sir—"

Mr. Rickets, or Richard as the gold plaque on his desk read, sat back with a sigh. "Miss Andrews, I can understand the stress the death of your parents caused you."

No, Richard, you really can't.

"And while we here at Pendleton want what's best for all our children, we cannot run the center without the tuition of each and every student."

"I understand. It's just that—"

"Do you have the money, Miss Andrews?"

Shit. "No. Not at the moment."

Richard, or Dick, as I'd begun to think of him, sighed again. "How long have you been stripping, Miss Andrews?"

Every inch of my body went cold. "I'm not a stripper, Mr. Rickets. I'm a waitress."

His condescending, pitying expression didn't escape my notice.

"You work at a gentleman's club."

"Yes."

"And what sort of role model do you think that makes you for Julian?"

My heart beat a staccato rhythm as I tried to hold back all the nasty, foulmouthed words I wanted to scream. The things I knew would get me nowhere. Still, it wasn't as if I had to sit back and take it.

"Do you have children, Richard?"

His lip twitched a bit at my use of his first name. "Yes, three."

"And how old were you when you had your oldest?"

"I'm not sure how—"

"Humor me, sir." I gave him my best work smile, the one that usually earned me an extra buck or two in tips.

He pursed his lips for a moment before answering in a curt tone. "Twenty-eight."

"And I assume you'd already completed your degree and established yourself in your career at that point."

"Miss Andrews—"

"You're taking my time, sir. You can at least allow me to

make my point."

Oooh, I'd hit a nerve if his glare was any indication. Lovely. Might as well go out with a bang.

"Yes," he said through gritted teeth. "You could say I was established in my career."

"Thank you." I sat back and crossed my legs, letting my foot dangle as I subtly adjusted my skirt up my thigh. Letting him get a good look because, deep down, I knew he wanted to. And I was never wrong about the desires of men. "I was twenty-two when my parents died. I had two more months of school left to finish my bachelor's degree and was working part time at a call center help desk. I didn't have the luxury of time I needed to establish myself anywhere when I was named guardian of Julian."

"Perhaps another family member would have been the better choice, then."

"Perhaps, though perhaps uprooting a young boy who'd just lost his parents and his sight in a single moment wouldn't have been the right thing. I know I didn't think it was. And while Julian and I were able to collect on my parents' life insurance, that money went toward the mortgage so we didn't have to move. Again, I didn't think uprooting Julian from the life he knew was the proper thing to do."

"Miss Andrews—"

Nope. Not done yet. "And while I'm sure from where you sit as the CFO of this institution, the realities of mortgages and groceries and taxes don't keep you up at night, but I can assure you, from the cheap seats at the back, those things do. Julian's tuition has been a priority from day one, but I spent too much time chasing a position in my field that would pay me enough as an entry-level employee for the two of us to survive. And you know what, sir? Those jobs are either hard to find or nonexistent in this economy. The tuition here ate up almost my entire salary, so I had to alter my plan."

He certainly didn't seem impressed. "And taking your clothes off for money seemed the responsible thing to do with an impressionable young man at home?"

"Once again, Richard, I don't strip. I waitress."

"In lingerie."

I shrugged, playing off my need to punch him in the throat. "It is a titty bar, sir."

"I don't appreciate your crassness, Charlotte."

"And I don't appreciate your judgment, Dick. I go to work like anyone else. I'm a dedicated employee and a professional in my field. Yes, I work at a strip club slinging drinks instead of at some multinational corporation taking phone calls on how to stop from crashing whatever program the user on the other end of the line needs to use. One isn't inherently better than the other until you look at the money made. Sure, I could toil away in a cube forty hours a week, put Julian into a public school that isn't equipped to deal with his special needs, and scrounge by with help from the local food pantry. Or I can wear clothing that covers more than most bathing suits while I smile at the patrons who come to watch a show and relax. It's as simple as that."

"Stripping is not as simple *as that*."

I'd always been amazed at how little some people heard, especially when a woman spoke. I uncrossed my legs and stood, rising slowly. Deliberately. Holding Dick's gaze the entire way.

"Once again, I'm not a stripper. I'm a waitress. And the fact that you can't understand the distinction makes me worry more about your influence as a role model to my brother than my job does."

I made it to the door before Dick decided to strike back.

"You have three weeks to pay the last installment of this year's tuition and the deposit for next year, Miss Andrews.

Otherwise, Julian won't be able to finish the semester."

I closed my eyes as my hand gripped the doorknob, a sinking feeling in my gut. Knowing there was no way, but unable to admit defeat.

"Understood, Mr. Rickets."

Time to hustle a little harder.

THREE

Rebel

"FERAL BREED BOSTON, WHAT say ye?"

The president of the Boston den stood and nodded his respect. "Down two, sir. Both to matings."

Blaze acknowledged the response with a nod before shuffling the papers in front of him, typical behavior from our leader during the quarterly club check-in.

"Look at these dens, losing members left and right to the love bite," Scab said softly, obviously trying not to interrupt the meeting still in progress. My newest fully patched den member may have been a bit of an old country boy, but he wasn't stupid. Blaze would cut him to the quick if he was dumb enough to cause a scene.

Jameson, a long-time friend and the President of the Four Corners den, sent Scab a low growl. "Matings are sacred and should be treated as such."

Scab upended his mug and guzzled the remaining ale. Most of it, at least. Some ran down the sides of his mouth and onto his shirt. We were going to have to have another talk about hygiene, it seemed.

And then the nasty fucker belched. "If they're so sacred,

there wouldn't be the rule where the new couple goes to fuck for three days while we guard their lazy asses and listen to everything they do."

"Scab," I warned, my own wolf releasing a throaty growl at our errant denmate. The dumbass was pushing buttons he should have known better than to play with.

"Please," Scab said, addressing me and ignoring Jameson. A stupid move on his part. "Like you didn't get hard listening to that guy from the Hollywood den and the fat whore he mated with? All that 'Oh, yes. Do it harder, spank me, yes. Get it, baby, get it.' I was hard for a week. Must have jacked to that soundtrack a hundred times so far. Bitch had the ass of a rhino, but it sure sounded like her cunt was—"

The crash of Jameson's fist into Scab's face brought a little attention our way, but not nearly as much as we would have garnered in a room full of humans. Wolf shifters were used to a show of violence now and again, especially those of us in the Feral Breed.

Jameson sat back with a snarl and reached for his drink, refocusing on the meeting going on across the room. As if throwing a punch was a daily occurrence and not anything to focus on. Which for such a rough, aggressive wolf shifter was probably the case.

Still, I gave him an arched brow and pointed my beer bottle at Scab's prone form. "You realize Blaze is probably going to take a stripe out of your ass for that after the meeting is over."

I knew why Jameson had hit the wretch, but that didn't mean Blaze would appreciate the distraction during den updates. As proven when the man in question glanced our way, one eyebrow raised.

"Feral Breed Buffalo, what say ye?"

Yeah, there'd be a reckoning later. Blaze—the National President of the Feral Breed Motorcycle Club, President of the

National Association of the Lycan Brotherhood or NALB, and the closest thing we had to a pack leader—could be as violent as any other wolf shifter. Only difference was, he had the primary position of power, so no wolf below him would fight back unless he was going for a direct challenge. Something I had yet to see.

Basically, Blaze was the man with the biggest balls in the room, and we were merely there to enact his laws and enforce his rules.

"Shit." Jameson scowled. "I hope Blaze agrees with me that the Rites of Klunzad are nothing to be joked about."

"He's Borzohn…of course, he will."

And therein lay the most basic difference between us. Borzohn wolves like Jameson, the ones born as shifters into a family pack, put much more stock in the centuries-old traditions their elders taught than those of us who'd been born and raised as humans before being turned. Anbizens usually had no patience for the antiquated ideals of packs that had been long decimated by war and prejudice. But the Borzohn shifters followed age-old rules like gospel, even when they made no sense in the modern world.

Though perhaps those rules were what kept them sane through their formative years as the wolf slowly took more control. Anbizens had the advantage of growing up human, so they tended to fit into society better than their Borzohn counterparts. But the Borzohn shared their body with the wolf spirit from birth. They tended to balance the man and beast better than us Anbizen.

Jameson curled his lip as Scab started to come to, apparently still pissed about what my den brother had said. "Boss man can take as many stripes as he wants. Scab here should be happy I was the one who got to him. Had any of the Hollywood den overheard his comment about their beloved pack sister, your pet Anbizen would be stuck in the med unit here at the Fields for the next month." He shot me a wicked grin. "And if her mate had heard him, Scab would be dead by now."

"There's no denying that. You never fuck with a wolf's mate."

We clinked our bottles in response. The belief that mates, the people the fates tied together before birth as perfect matches for one another, were more than just bed warmers or broodmares was something we agreed on. Something other shifters from both sides of the birth lines chose not to believe.

Blaze focused his attention on our corner of the room. "Feral Breed Four Corners, what say ye?"

Jameson stood and nodded once in response. "No losses, sir. Our club is static at forty-six members split evenly between a northern and southern den."

"And the denhouse in Flagstaff? Have the repairs been completed?"

Jameson paused. The grinding of his teeth coincided with the way he curled his hands into fists. "Not yet, sir. I expect completion within two weeks."

Blaze peered at Jameson from the dais at the front of the room. "Have the vandals been located?"

"We're still tracking them, sir," Jameson bit out, hair sprouting at the back of his neck as he fought his shift. The wolf in him had to be boiling mad. It was an inherent risk when in a room full of Alpha wolves. The slightest challenge could set off a violent outburst. That's why the club-style leadership of our individual regions worked so well. Voted presidents such as Jameson and myself, vice presidents, Sergeants-at-Arms... every man had his job and his place. It kept the violence to a minimum.

Sure there were other groups with the same structure— military-style band of brother types came to mind—but motorcycle clubs were decidedly human and relatively normal in average America. We fit in well enough, and the negative connotations of a group of men in black leather riding motorcycles together tended to influence most humans to keep a little distance from us. Plus, our wolves got off on the feeling of riding a motorcycle. There was a freedom to it, something impossible to duplicate when stuck inside a box on wheels. If we couldn't four-paw a trip, we wanted to do it on two wheels with nothing separating our senses from the world around us.

But place us in a room filled with other teams and the leader of the whole wolf population of North America? Even the strongest shifter would have trouble keeping his wolf at bay. As showcased by Jameson's shaking as Blaze stared him down.

And Blaze would win. "I want them found, Jameson. They have desecrated a den of the Feral Breed. I desire justice."

Jameson offered Blaze a tight nod. "No more than I do, sir."

Blaze stood quiet for a moment, his eyes hard and locked with Jameson's. My wolf perked up at the tension between the two. He pushed his way to the front of my mind, ears pricked and eyes watchful. My hand gripped the bottle tighter as the human side of me prepared for a mental fight. I couldn't get involved if Jameson challenged Blaze. Doing so could mean death or banishment, depending upon the outcome of the battle. But my wolf liked to jump into a good fight, and he had a tendency to do so whether my human side agreed or not.

Thankfully, there would be no fight to resist joining.

Blaze snapped his teeth once, making the entire room stiffen up. Jameson immediately dropped his gaze and sat down, chastised as it was. My wolf settled back down as well, though he waited until the tension broke and Blaze went back to shuffling his papers. I set my bottle on the table and opened my hand, stretching the tendons back out. Claw-like tips to my fingers faded back to standard human form, but my skin burned under my jeans and leather cut. A sure sign of how close my wolf had been to demanding we take his form. Had Jameson not submitted when he did, my joints would be aching with the need to shift. A feeling that would need to be alleviated.

Giving myself over to my wolf form was the easiest way to relieve the tension racing through my veins, though it was not my preferred method. I'd need another hit of The Draught, the drug I'd formulated to quiet those damnable wolf instincts, or a bit of balls-deeping before the night was over if I had any hope of staying in my human form the next time the mangy fucker inside of me decided to try to rule.

"Moving on," Blaze said, his voice rougher than his normal tone. "Feral Breed Great Lakes, what say ye?"

I stood and offered Blaze a nod, fighting not to vocalize the snarl my wolf wanted to give our leader. "Sir, we have no losses to report this quarter. We've added two new wolves to our club, bringing our membership to forty-two shifters divided into eastern and western divisions."

Blaze glanced down at his notes. "I see the two additions are recently turned Anbizen wolves. How are they assimilating?"

I glanced at Scab, still unconscious on the floor. I wouldn't have called his turning recent; he'd been a shifter for nearly sixty years. But an ancient such as Blaze would certainly view the years a bit differently than his far-younger counterpart.

"They're learning their places, sir."

Blaze's brow furrowed until he followed my gaze to the lump of man on the floor. He grimaced. "Yes, well, some men take longer than others."

He shuffled his papers, humming for a moment until he found what he was looking for. "There's been a report of a woman turning up at a Milwaukee hospital with claw marks on her body. Just the one case so far, and she claims to not remember what caused the injury. But the story is enough to garner the attention of the local NALB regional head. I'd like your crew to head there and investigate the issue. Make sure we don't have a man-eating nomad on our hands."

"Of course, sir. I can roll out my team as soon as the meeting is through."

Blaze locked his eyes with mine, causing a low whine to escape my throat. My wolf may have been dominant by nature, but his dominance didn't compare to that of a shifter such as Blaze. With five hundred-plus years of life behind him, Blaze had more than twice as much time as I did honing his power and aggression.

"With the location so close to the Fields, I would find it allowable for you and your den members to be excused from the meeting early. I can have Half Trac send you the final meeting notes."

Not wanting to start a challenge, I broke eye contact. "Whatever you require."

"Perfect. Thank you, Rebel." He grunted and looked down to the papers stacked on the podium, shuffling as if to find the next crew. "Feral Breed Heartland, what say ye?"

I shot a look over to Gates, the road captain for this trip. He gave me a quick nod before he turned and exited the room. No doubt he'd collect the rest of my men, minus the still unconscious Scab. The brothers of my den were strong and efficient; they'd be ready to hit the road as soon as I said "ride." Merriweather Fields sat only an hour south of Milwaukee, a giant colonial-style mansion northwest of Chicago that had been home to the President of the NALB for decades. We'd be investigating before nightfall.

Scab's groaning interrupted my thoughts, and I found myself scowling down at the fallen man. "You know, Jameson, next time you might want to go easy on the poor fellow."

"And what fun would that be?"

The man had a point. "Not a whole hell of a lot." I grinned and finished my beer.

Scab finally pulled himself to his feet, his club cut askew and one hell of a nasty bruise already forming on his jaw. As shifters, we healed faster than human men and were pretty damned hard to kill, but a full-strength punch from a fellow wolf shifter was enough to do some damage.

As Gates returned from where the lesser patched members were congregated, Scab spit on the floor and shot Jameson as nasty glare. Gates snarled in response, obviously unhappy with Scab's behavior. With his black hair and bright blue eyes, Gates tended to wear the "pretty boy" moniker like a shroud and be underestimated for it. But he was trained to kill in more ways than I could count, and his wolf was a strong tactician, which was why I'd named him Sergeant-at-Arms. Fighter, enforcer, and the man who kept the rest of our members in line—that was Gates' role. And he took his responsibilities seriously.

"The team's ready to roll out."

I nodded toward Scab. "Throw his sled in the back of the war wagon and make him follow us up there. I don't want to have to explain the loss of a member due to his own idiocy."

Gates smirked, a rare sight on the normally stoic shifter. "Understood."

He grabbed Scab by the arm and half dragged him from the meeting room. Idiot that he was, Scab cursed and blubbered the entire way, causing much more of a scene than he should have. I'd have to do something soon to knock the attitude out of him. He'd been pushing the limits of respect for too long, and I'd let him get away with it because I understood the battle between man and wolf in Anbizen shifters. But as the president of our den, it would be my job to remind Scab of the proper way to interact with fellow shifters. And I'd give his reminder with teeth and claws instead of words.

The roar of four engines coming to life outside interrupted the relative silence of the meeting hall. The sound called to me, made me crave the throaty rumble of the Boardwalk I'd driven out from Detroit. If I couldn't have a willing woman under me, at least I could have the power of my favorite small cruising bike between my legs.

"That's my cue." I reached across the table and clasped Jameson's forearm. "Ride hard, my brother."

"Keep it shiny side up. And good luck above the cheese curtain, my friend."

I straightened my cut and grinned. "I'm a two-hundred-plus-year-old wolf shifter, a member of the Feral Breed, and the president of my fucking den. I don't need luck."

FOUR

SIX HOURS AFTER LEAVING Dick's office, I was fighting back a growl as another customer pinched my ass. Did no man ever follow the rules? I turned to remind the pincher that he wasn't allowed to touch, but the face smiling at me was one of my regulars. Daresay, one of my favorites, if a waitress in a strip club could have a favorite customer.

Old Ben Miller had been coming here for years, rolling into the club on his Rascal nearly every night. He spent his retirement money on watered-down drinks and attention from any girl willing to look past his frail body and horndog attitude to the twenties he offered. Which were many of us, if not all. Money disguised a multitude of problems.

His half-toothless grin slashed across his face in a crooked line. "Cherry, baby. When're you gonna get up on the stage and shake that thing for me?"

God, the nicknames the owner gave us girls. Cherry…as in virginal. As in so not me. I forced my lips into a smile. The man asked me that question at least once every shift, and I always gave him the same answer.

"Now, Ben. You know Mr. Morris only likes the skinny

girls dancing the pole." I leaned over as if to whisper to him, giving him a good view of my cleavage. "He thinks these curves will get y'all too excited."

As expected, Old Ben tucked a bill into the cup of my bra and gave me a wink.

"I can still get it up, you know. Don't even need none of that Viagra."

Pleasant thoughts, for sure. "Good for you, Ben."

The overhead speaker crackled before the DJ's voice thundered through the room.

"And now, on the main stage, get ready to make it rain with Dynasty!"

Ben's watery eyes locked on the pole where Dynasty would be dancing in about ten seconds. "Oh, now she's got a real nice set of titties on her."

And my work with him was done. "She sure does. You make sure you tip her well for giving you a show, okay? Have fun, Ben."

Lord, to have all my customers be as kind and generous as old Ben. That would be a dream gig. Ben didn't break the rules much, didn't manhandle or demand. A little pinch occasionally, a brush of his fingers a bit too close to a nipple now and again, but otherwise he was a gentleman. A rare species in this place.

I visually checked on my tables as I walked away, making sure to shake my hips with every step. Might as well earn those tips as I was making sure the house got theirs with the drink money. I'd learned early on how to get a feel for a group of patrons, how to spot the good ones from the ones who would cause trouble. It was a skill that came in handy even outside the club, and one I was glad to have mastered. Silver lining, and all that. Working at a strip club had never exactly been on my list of career choices, but when life hands you lemons, you make lemonade. Or you tuck those bad boys in your bra and learn to shake it like the girls working in this dump did.

"Anything you boys need?" I smiled at the two young men at table three and cocked my hip as I'd been trained to do. Anything to draw attention to "the assets," as my boss loved to say. Skinny, flexible, willing-to-get-naked girls made bank on the stages, though not out on the floor. Those of us with a little more meat on our bones, a few more soft curves to grab hold of, went home with the most tips out of the waitresses. And I had soft curves to spare.

Guy number one definitely seemed to appreciate those curves as he looked me up and down. "I'll have a gin and tonic. Matt? Yo, Matt."

The second guy at the table finally looked up. *Shit.* Eyes glassy and unfocused, a flush to his face that betrayed the air conditioning in the place, and a shakiness to his movements all made my jaw clench. I had a drunk on my hands.

"How about I get Matt here a nice glass of ice water or a cup of coffee?" I turned to leave the table but stopped when someone grabbed me by the hip from behind.

"Where ya going, beautiful? I got a lap you can sit on right here." Drunk Matt laughed and turned to his friend, still with his hand. On. My. Body. "I've got a lot more she could sit on down here as well."

I smacked his hand off my hip, scanning for security as subtly as possible. Drunk guys in this place were trouble for sure; drunk younger guys could be downright dangerous. Matt fell into the dangerous category if his baby face was any indication of his age.

"Now, boys." I sugared up my voice even as I made sure to stand out of the danger zone. No sense giving up tips if I didn't have to. "I'm sure the bouncer at the door told you the rules when you walked in. No touching unless I touch first. And absolutely no lap dances from the waitstaff. I'd be more than happy to find you one of the dancers if that's what you're looking for."

"Fuck the dancers. I want your big ass bouncing on my cock." Drunk Matt thrust his hips off the seat of his chair as he jerked his arms up and down.

So very charming.

"Sorry, Matt. But my big ass and I are not for sale. Now let me get you your drinks."

Drunk Matt laughed again. "Yeah, bitch. Get me something to put in my mouth. I'll make it worth your while."

He flicked his tongue, something I'd never once in my life understood. Who found that shit attractive? Certainly not me. My hands shook with the need to flee as I turned and left the two behind. This day had gone from bad to worse, that was for sure. Face burning and fighting the urge to scream, I strode to the bar to do the job I was being paid to do, even though I'd reached my bullshit limit already. I was so damned tired of this place.

But no money, no tuition for Julian, so I needed to dig deep and keep smiling. "G and T and a Folgers, please."

Caleb, one of our newest bartenders, glanced up from the drink he'd been mixing. I shivered and took a reflexive step back as his eyes met mine. Those eyes were the creepiest shade of green—unnaturally pale, the irises nearly washed out. The unusual color and huge red scar running across his cheekbone made the hair on the back of my neck stand up every time he looked at me. Or maybe it was the way he looked at me like I was something to eat.

And my God, did he seem hungry.

Caleb smirked, his top lip curling over his canine teeth in a way that spoke of aggression, of predator versus prey. And by the look on his face, he knew exactly how uncomfortable he made me.

"Whatever the lady needs."

Creepy didn't even begin to describe him. "Yeah. Thanks."

"Hey, girl." Chanel saved me from making small talk with my nightmares as she approached the bar. Armed with a killer smile and a swagger that held men's attention like no other, the woman was a veritable dynamo at the club. Her huge rack didn't hold her back, either. She was also one of the kindest, most naturally happy people I'd ever met. If she weren't my best work friend, I'd hate her.

"Hi, Chanel. How're the boys?"

She gave me a wink before nodding toward Caleb. "Two rum and diets, a sex on the beach, and a bucket of lights." Once she finished her order, she grinned, directing that sunny grin my way. "Oh lord, David is driving me to drinking. I swear that boy is seven going on seventeen. But little Michael is my perfect baby still. He got two new teeth this past week and barely even made a peep about it."

"Two teeth?" I tutted and shook my head. "That's crazy. You tell that baby to stop growing."

"I wish." She sighed and brushed a piece of hair off her face. "How's Julian doing? You convince those blowhards at his school to help you find some sort of financial aid for him or something yet?"

My smile froze, turning plastic in an instant. *Money... Julian...make the money...keep Julian in school. Shit.* "Um, no. Not yet, but I'm working on it. Oh, there's my order. See ya later."

I grabbed the tray of drinks Caleb set on the counter and hurried away. It was never easy talking about Julian and the reality of my raising him. All my coworkers knew about the accident, but none of them fully understood what Julian went through every day. None of them had ever been around a kid who'd lost the use of one of his senses in an instant. The abrupt change was agonizing and cruel, and the school teaching him a new way to navigate the world cost a fortune. Hence my working at a strip club and my discussion with Dick-Richard-Rickets earlier in the day. The one that got me nowhere, as usual.

The degree I'd earned in Computer Information Systems didn't do me a lot of good once I realized how crappy the places hiring paid. When the crowds were decent, I'd make more in tips in a weekend than I made in a week sitting behind a computer in a cube. Lessons learned and all that.

But still, it wasn't quite enough to pay tuition at Pendleton. Not without a hell of a lot more hustle, at least.

The rest of the night was pretty much the same—deliver drinks, flirt, wipe down tables, smile, do my best not to smack the handsy jerks who didn't follow the rules, flirt some more. By the end of my shift, my feet hurt, my back ached, and I reeked of beer due to a clumsy drunk and a full drink tray. But I had a bra full of twenties and the hope that, with a few more nights like this one, I'd at least have enough to pay what I owed to Pendleton for the current school year. Next year...well, I'd have to try a little harder still.

I walked off the floor at the end of my shift with a stride that had me eating up the distance between me and freedom. There was nothing I wanted more than a shower, a pair of flannel pajama pants, and my bed. I had another long shift the next night, and I wanted to be well-rested and ready to work the room hard. Julian needed that school, which meant I needed to earn some cash.

I had almost reached the changing room when I heard my least favorite sound in the world. The danger of being forced past the boss' office.

"Cherry, I need a girl for a party." The manager of Amnesia Gentlemen's Club sat behind his desk, which was covered in dirty magazines and even dirtier ashtrays. Those smoking bans the state had enacted didn't apply to him, apparently.

Taking a deep breath and hoping like hell for a miracle, I leaned into the open doorway. "I'm sorry, Mr. Morris, but my shift just ended."

"I don't remember phrasing those words as a question, Cherry." He glared at me, turning my blood to ice. I tried to avoid him most days because, like Caleb, there was something too aggressive about him. He gave me the major creeps. I didn't understand why I always struggled with a fight-or-flight response to them both, but I did. And I usually preferred the flight option. Apparently, that wouldn't be an option tonight.

"Yes, sir," I said, my voice a little quieter than normal. *Focus on Julian and school. On money. You can make it through.* "I appreciate the work. I'll just go get ready for the party."

"Good girl. And, Cherry? Clean up a little, will you? I need my girls pristine for this group. They'll be here in ten minutes, so don't take long." He returned to his paperwork, probably waiting for the next unlucky employee to walk by.

I clenched my jaw as my hand curled into a fist behind me. "Of course, Mr. Morris."

I thought I'd escaped, but as I walked away, he yelled, "And wear the blue panty set. It makes your ass look fantastic."

Typical. The blue panty set barely covered my ass. Of course, he'd want me to wear that. I sighed as I shoved open the changing room door. If I was lucky, I'd have time to shower, grab a bottle of water, and scarf down a sandwich from the kitchen before having to hit the floor again. Luckily, Julian was at a friend's house for the night, so at least I didn't need to worry about him while I worked the party. And perhaps I'd even make enough tonight to start paying down next year's tuition. I'd love to walk into Pendleton with enough cash to get Julian to graduation and tell Mr. Rickets where to shove his judgment.

Eight minutes and a costume change later, I waited in the largest of the three private rooms at the back of the club. The rooms offered comfortable seating for our guests, a private stage, one personal waitress, and the renter's choice of two girls to entertain them. A nice enough setup, and yet I hated working the private parties. Unlike the rest of the club, there were no cameras, and the only rule the girls had to follow was to make sure the customer left happy. From what I'd seen in the past, that included lap dances, hand jobs, and blow jobs on a regular night. On a more exotic night, when the party host paid for a "special event," things could get a little too kinky for my taste. Blood play, breath play; I'd even witnessed a foursome involving one dancer and three groomsmen.

Nothing really shocked me anymore.

Rules regarding waitresses stayed in place, though. No touching unless we touched first, no nakedness offered, and no lap dances allowed. Another reason why I stayed a waitress. The tips as a dancer were nice, but there was no way I could go home to my fifteen-year-old brother after doing any of *that*.

Of course, Julian knew where I worked. There were no secrets between us, not since our parents died four years ago and left us alone with only each other for support. He knew all about my job choices and why I decided to be a waitress at Amnesia. But at least I could hold my head up when I got home, could tell him honestly about my shift without having to worry he'd ever find out something that would make him feel ashamed of me.

It was the one consolation in my shitty little life.

The sound of men's voices and heavy footsteps moving closer set my heart to racing. And so it begins…

Star tiptoed in through the back door of the room and stepped on stage. "Showtime."

I nodded, ready to support the dancers as best I could. We

all benefited from happy customers in a situation like this, so working together was sort of a no-brainer.

Porsche, the second assigned dancer, I assumed, opened the door off the main hallway with a flourish and a giggle before leading in a group of men. Big men, rough ones with leather vests and coats on. Motorcycle club members.

Wonderful.

Knowing this party could potentially get a little out of control with the type of clientele involved, I sent up a quick prayer for an easy night, nothing too off the wall, and a bouncer who took the rules seriously. The last thing I needed was to have fight one of these guys by myself.

Still, they were customers. And customers meant tips. So I put on my best smile, ready to flirt. Ready to earn those bills.

A tall blond man in a dark gray T-shirt and leather vest walked through the door last. Gorgeous, utterly delicious, and totally sin incarnate; those descriptions flew through my head as I took in the muscles, the wavy hair, and the tight-as-fuck jeans. But when he turned my way and met my stare, my knees nearly buckled. One look into those sky-colored eyes and my body responded. Within a single heartbeat, I was dripping wet and ready to throw him on the floor so I could have my way with him.

Well, shit.

FIVE

"SO BASICALLY WE THROW a party and get lap dances." Scab held his hand up as if Gates was supposed to high-five him. My Sergeant-at-Arms simply glared until the other shifter gave up.

Meanwhile, I was trying my best not to smack the fucker upside the back of the head. Scab wasn't going to survive this trip if he kept being a dumbass. He'd been far too excited about this plan ever since we discovered the woman who'd been clawed had been an employee at a gentlemen's club between Milwaukee and the Illinois border.

I never should have told him that part. "This isn't a party. We've booked a private room so we can determine how this woman ended up with claw marks."

Scab shrugged. "Sounds like a party. God, I hope they've got a blonde with a big ass. I haven't had a good lap dance in weeks."

"Have a little respect, you cretin," Gates said with a growl. "If there's a nomad in the area, these women are in danger. And if the authorities catch wind of this guy before we find him, we as a species are in danger."

Scab walked right up into the face of the snarling sergeant, a definite challenge. "You know, Gates, if you'd get a little pussy now and again, you'd be in a much better mood. You've got this whole *GQ* model thing going for you. The ladies totally fall all over themselves trying to shove their tits in your face, but you do nothing. You're failing all mankind by not taking those lovely ladies up on as many offers as you can physically handle. Get out there and take advantage of it. Even a pretty wolf like you needs to get his dick wet now and again."

Gates loomed over Scab, lip curled and hands clenched into fists. Seeming to grow wider and taller with the building of his rage. The tension in the air grew thick, the rest of my team responding with various low growls and muscle twitches as they fought the urge to shift. My wolf didn't react. He'd established his dominance over Gates long ago. These men were no challenge to our authority, but that didn't mean he wasn't enjoying the power play.

Scab held his ground, though. Holding eye contact with an effort that showed in the way his hands shook and the sweat beaded on his brow. The growls flying back and forth grew louder, the vibrations rougher. The lesser wolf had a serious stake in this fight, a chance at a real challenge, it seemed. Not that I wanted that. Gates would kill without regret if Scab didn't break his stare and settle back into his place.

Luckily for him, the Scab's wolf forced him to acknowledge his lower status. He broke his stare and took a step back, giving Gates some room. Not that that was what Gates wanted. My sergeant followed Scab's steps, stalking him, hunting him as he retreated. Finally, probably fearful Gates would attack even though he was no longer a threat, Scab turned his head, baring his neck to the victor of the little challenge.

Gates barely acknowledged the concession, which was better than most wolves. They'd rub the defeat in Scab's face.

The larger shifter merely huffed and leaned against the van parked behind him.

"I'm not interested in getting my dick wet," Gates said, his voice like ice, a dangerous clip to his words. "But thanks for the advice."

"Suit yourself." Scab shrugged and stepped away, his voice rough and his movements jerky. If I had to guess, he and his wolf didn't agree on the conflict resolution. I'd need to watch him closely around Gates to make sure he didn't try to go all sneaky-fucker. Sliding in through a back door and taking the better man by surprise. That kind of bullshit could tear a den apart. We needed to have faith that our brothers respected us and had our backs, no matter what.

"So, what's the plan?" Shadow, our team medic, asked. Every head whipped in his direction even though no one responded. I was pretty sure no one knew *what* to say. The kid rarely spoke.

I glanced at Gates, who was watching the young shifter with a smirk on his face. Gates had a soft spot for the wolf we'd recently voted to patch into the group. Shadow had been our prospect for two years before he'd earned his road name and his colors during a raid on a gang of wolves selling a homemade version on The Draught. Because the chemical formula of the only drug known to calm our inner beasts was my creation— and something we made a great deal of money selling—we took piracy seriously. Shadow had fought as hard as the rest of us to shut the illegal operation down. And he'd shown true stealth, sneaking past multiple guard stations along the way. He was our ninja, our shadow warrior.

And suddenly he was speaking without being asked a direct question.

With one last glance around my motley crew, I crossed my arms and lifted my chin. "We go in, pretend to be having a celebration, and scope out the scene. If there are pack wolves, we talk to them. If there are nomads, we end them. Over and done."

THE SIX OF US strolled through the front door of the club precisely as planned, joking and roughhousing like a normal group of human men about to celebrate. But that's where the good-time show ended. Our senses were all on high alert—our wolf sides listening, watching, and smelling. They had to. If there was something wrong here, we needed to figure it out and eradicate the problem.

A man I recognized as a shifter belonging to the Milwaukee pack met us as we entered. Monroe...Morrison...Moskal. What was his name?

"Well, if it isn't the Feral Breed. What an honor to have you here tonight. I'm Mr. Morris, the manager of Amnesia Gentlemen's Club. How can we be of service?"

Morris. Of course. Cousin of the pack Alpha and all-around suck-up. Right. Gates stepped forward, taking the lead as I knew he would.

"Our brother Scab here is celebrating a birthday." The sergeant grabbed Scab around the neck, hitting him a little harder than he probably needed to. "We thought we'd throw him a little party since we're passing through town."

Scab jerked forward, probably nudged by Gates in some way that would make me cackle when I found out. "Yeah. We heard you've got some interesting talent here."

Morris grinned, the expression oddly snakelike for a wolf shifter. "Oh, yes, the talent here is exceptional."

"Perfect." Gates released Scab and clasped Morris on the arm, directing him farther into the club. Leading him away from the rest of us, again, as planned. "We reserved a room under the name of Woodward."

I led the rest of the group through the club, following Morris and Gates at enough of a distance not to be noticed by the manager. I caught the scents of six different wolves along the way, but that wasn't immediately concerning. The club was located a little off the beaten path on a stretch of highway that led to the local pack's territory. Shifters in a local bar would be par for the course.

But when I walked into the private room we reserved, every hair on my body stood on end. My nerves fired in pulses, sending anticipatory tingles all over my body. Something was coming, something big. It was as if lightning was about to strike right in front of me, and I had nowhere to run. Mouth dry and hands clammy, I glanced around the room while my wolf howled in my head.

And then I was gone.

Blond, beautiful, with bright green eyes locked on mine. A woman who intrigued, entranced, and aroused.

Mate.

My wolf whined and huffed as my mind spun. I'd never even contemplated the possibility of meeting my mate, figuring I'd die early as most unmated shifters did. Yet there she was, all soft and light and absolutely fucking perfect. I wanted to grab her. I wanted to kiss her, bite her, lick her skin. I wanted to bury my face in her breasts and hold on to her hips as I rutted against her. I wanted to fuck her through the floor then soothe her delicate pussy with my tongue.

I wanted not to be caught in a room full of half-naked women with my cock about to burst through the fly of my jeans.

"Shit," I hissed, willing my body to stand down. Gates caught my eye, seemingly concerned, but I shook him off. I couldn't deal with explanations right then.

"Gentlemen, please meet the ladies who will be at your

service tonight." Morris moved through the room, doing a good job of a Vanna White impersonation as he introduced each woman. "This is Star and the lovely Porsche; they'll be dancing for you tonight. And this beautiful lady will be your private waitress. Say hello, Cherry."

I could hardly control the need to flash my canines as Morris wrapped his fingers around Cherry's arm and pulled her to the center of the room.

My mate. Our mate.

A hand landed on my shoulder, restraining and heavy. I whipped my head around and growled.

"Take it easy, man," Gates whispered.

Shit. I checked on each guy in turn. None seemed to have noticed whatever Gates had, though I thought I saw Cherry glancing at me out of the corner of her eye. Had I scared her? I only wanted to keep Morris' greasy hands off her. Keep every other man's hands off my mate.

Jesus…I had a mate.

"Let's get this party started." Scab clapped his hands and took a seat toward the front, ready for his lap dances. Morris left with nothing more than a whisper to Gates, and the women got to work.

My guys made themselves comfortable at the tables while I hung out in the back on a couch that reeked of sweat and sex. What the hell happened back here? *Fuck.* I ran a hand down my face and tried to calm my aching cock. I knew exactly what happened back here. And God help me if one of my men tried to make that happen with my Cherry.

I silently tracked her all night, following her with my eyes as she took orders and handed out drinks. The way she smiled and flirted, the way she swung her hips when she walked, how her ass jiggled in those barely there little short things that looked as if they were meant to be worn under her clothes. She was sin and sex and all kinds of wrong wrapped up in one gorgeous package.

But I couldn't make a move to introduce myself. She was my lust personified but nothing I could have at that moment. She was a mere human, and we had a possible man-eating wolf on our hands who was a danger to humans. Case first, mate second.

And then what?

As Star bent over and shook her bare ass in Scab's face, something that had the guys laughing and hollering, I sat in the back and watched as my world fell apart. Being mated meant leaving the Feral Breed. No mated wolf rode, not a single one stayed on once they met their fated match. I would have to give up my job and my brothers to have my mate. I'd be trading a lifestyle I'd loved and honored for decades for a future with someone I hadn't even met yet. My wolf was positive she was the one for us, but the man wasn't happy about losing everything he cherished for a woman.

And didn't that just chap my ass.

"What do you need, darlin'?"

"You."

The answer burst from my lips, automatic and unintended. I hadn't even noticed Cherry approaching, too caught up in my thoughts. But there she was, looking right at me, and good lord, I could smell her. A little scared, a little anxious, and a whole hell of a lot aroused. My wolf liked that last smell best, licking his jowls and preening as our mate smiled at us.

"I'm not on the menu tonight, handsome. How about a beer?"

I bit my lip as my cock again grew to full mast. Her proximity made me crazy; her honeyed scent drove my wolf mad. The wolf's needs were simple—sleep, food, fuck. The man...well, my needs were partially in line with my wolf's, plus a few more.

Like my brothers, my bikes, and my commitment to the Breed.

Like my need to beat the shit out of Scab if he didn't stop looking at my Cherry's ass.

"I'll take a light beer, thanks." I kept my eyes on hers as I released a subtle growl. The sound shouldn't have been loud enough for a human to hear, but a wolf, especially one of my own, would respond to the threat.

Much to my surprise, Scab completely ignored me while Cherry's eyes grew wide.

"What is that?" she asked, her voice low. The scent of her desire increased, and her face flushed an enticing shade of pink. The woman enveloped me in her desire, making me rock hard and ready to roll over for a little of her attention. Preferably focused on my cock.

I licked my lips. "You heard that?"

She nodded, her eyes still staring into mine. I couldn't decide if I should be thrilled my mate could hear my wolf sounds or terrified. There would be no way to hide my shifter side. I'd have to tell her almost immediately, giving me no time to court her first. Did people even court anymore? It wasn't as if I'd dated in the last hundred years or so. Unmated shifters didn't date—we fucked. There was no point in doing the whole relationship bullshit when finding a mate could end things with a single glance. I had no idea how to entice a woman to want to spend time with me that didn't involve getting her off.

My mind was entirely focused on Cherry and the battle raging within me, so at first I didn't catch the way my brothers grew quiet or the stillness in the room.

Until I smelled the blood.

One whiff and the reality of why we were at the club slammed me back into work mode. Glancing around the room, I noticed Numbers whispering to Shadow and Pup. My three younger wolves stood close together, their eyes bouncing from door to door as they scanned for possible threats. Scab had both strippers completely naked and writhing all over him, but his eyes kept cutting to Gates. My Sergeant-at-Arms sat board-straight on a couch to my left, taking in the entire scene with his trademark expressionless face. They all smelled the blood.

We needed to get out of this room and find the source, but first, I needed to make sure my mate was safe.

My mate…right smack-dab in the middle of this bullshit. Fuck.

"Hey, Cherry?" I kept my voice soft but with a slight growl to it. She seemed to like the sound, and I really needed her to accept what I was about to ask her to do.

Cherry made a humming noise, throaty and almost purr-like in tone. If I hadn't been afraid of her being in the same building with a possible man-eater, I probably would have thrown her down and rutted against her for the hotness of that sound. I wanted her to make it all night, every night, and I wanted to be the cause of it.

But all thoughts of the possibility of getting Cherry underneath me fled when a roar thundered through the building.

"Pup!" I was on my feet in an instant, my hand on Cherry's arm and my claws ready to come out.

The youngest member of my den, an unpatched prospect who'd been a hanger-on for the past year, rushed to my side. "Yes, boss?"

"Get the women out of here and put them somewhere out of the way. I want them safe." With a snarl and a flash of teeth, I placed Cherry's hand in his. "Especially her."

SIX

"IN YOU GO, LADIES." The young man who'd been told to put us somewhere out of the way directed the three of us into the changing room. Star trembled and grabbed the first robe she found to cover her naked body while Porsche strode in with a scowl on her pretty face.

I, on the other hand, trudged along slowly, wanting so badly to see that blond biker again. "How long are we going to be stuck in here?"

The look the man shot my way, the intensity behind his eyes, sent chills up my spine. I slunk back, huddling closer to Star. The kid who'd been called Pup stared at me as if I was on display, as if inspecting me for something. The coldness of his eyes belied his youthful face and shaggy hair. This was no young surfer-wannabe.

"You'll be in here as long as it takes. I'll be right outside the door." He looked me over again, his eyes pausing on my breasts. "You might want to put some clothes on."

Without another word, he left the room.

"Well, ain't this a crock of shit?" Porsche banged her locker open. "I could have been making bank out on the floor, but no, those bikers had to get all 'Oooh, something's going on. Let's get you weak little women to safety.' And what's with the whole 'especially Cherry' thing? You know these guys?"

Heart racing, throat tight, I answered the only way I could. Honestly. "I've never met them before."

But I want to.

"The one with the blond hair sure seemed as if he knew you." Star walked past me on her way to her locker, still a little pale and shaky. "He couldn't keep his eyes off you all night. I thought he was going to bite my head off when I offered him a beej while you were snagging drinks."

Something close to fury raged through me. "You did what?"

She shrugged, casual and unconcerned about my glare. "I offered him a blow job. I figured it'd be a quick fifty bucks. The man was pitching a major tent when I approached, but apparently, I wasn't what he had in mind." She looked over her shoulder and raised her eyebrows at me. "He turned me down and just kept watching you work the room."

Huh.

"I have no idea why he turned you down." I licked my lips to hide the smile trying to sneak across my face. It was oddly satisfying to know he had probably watched me as much as I watched him. *Double huh.*

"I'm glad that party's over." Porsche huffed as she pulled her jeans up her thighs. "Those guys creeped me out."

I nodded because they were a bit creepy.

Most of them, at least.

Rebel

GATES, NUMBERS, AND I left the private room in search of the club manager. I sent Scab and Shadow to the main room in case everything went sideways. They'd need to get the humans out of the building before anyone went full-on wolf.

Which was what I wanted to do the second I saw my prey. "Morris!"

The man turned, his annoyed expression morphing into that reptilian smile in a heartbeat. But I hadn't missed it. Greasy motherfucker was up to something.

"How can I help you, sir?"

"Name's Rebel, and I get the feeling my brothers and I are missing out on one hell of a party." I tapped the side of my nose and raised my eyebrows. There was no way the guy wouldn't have understood I was indicating the scent of blood permeating the place.

But apparently, he was going to try.

"I have no idea what you mean." Morris stood a little straighter but looked away. The chickenshit.

But really, two could play at that game. I gave the man a predatory smile and smacked Gates on the chest. "You hear this? As if we can't smell it." I growled and stalked closer, my grin turning wicked as Morris backed into the wall. "Blood and sex go well together, don't you think?"

"Ah, yes. Well…" Morris frantically glanced up and down the hall as if looking for anyone who could overhear before he leaned closer and dropped his voice. "We do *occasionally* offer exclusive parties to some of our more discerning guests."

Jackpot. "By discerning you mean angry, hungry, and horny, right? Because I'm pretty sure that describes my entire party."

Gates and Numbers joined me in caging Morris in, each one looming over the sputtering shifter.

Morris paled. "Sir, these parties are planned months in advance. The girls are hand-selected to be of the utmost perfection for what the host prefers. This isn't something I can put together on short notice. Now, if you'd like to—"

I growled, long and deep. His teeth snapped audibly with the force of him shutting his trap.

"What I'd like is to get in on the action happening—" I sniffed, pinpointing the source as close as I could without tracking it farther along the hall "—downstairs, perhaps?"

"It's not possible," Morris practically whispered, his face pale and his skin clammy. Scared. The man was truly scared. Interesting.

The sound of footfalls from another shifter reached my ears before he reached the corner. I was ready with a glare and a growl when the stranger walked up on us.

"What's the problem?" Tall, massive, with ice-green eyes and a wicked scar to rival my denmate Beast's deformed mug, this shifter gave off the air of someone pissed and ready to fight. That was okay with me. After the whole "my mate, can't have a mate, others staring at my mate" shit, I could use a little relaxation-by-fist.

"These gentlemen would like to join the party downstairs." Morris practically hissed the last word.

Iceman met my gaze. He didn't outright challenge me, but he definitely didn't back down to my glare. I cocked an eyebrow and waited, doubting he had the balls to attack. Few did.

But this wasn't some young pup with something to prove. Iceman smirked and brought his hand to his mouth in a way that screamed calculation. The scent of blood surrounded him, unmistakable even though the maroon stains around his fingernails had dried. Numbers growled behind me, but I kept my focus on the beast. He held my gaze as he stuck his tongue out and lapped at the remaining traces of blood on his fingers.

The man was one filthy motherfucker. Filthy…and persistent.

Tired of enduring his attempt at intimidation, I called my wolf forward, welcoming the burn and pull as I allowed a slow shift to begin. Shifting forms in a precise and calculated order was something few wolves could manage, the level of control needed too far out of their grasp. But if there was one thing I had above others, it was excellent fucking control. So I let the huge shifter get a look at a real Alpha ready to attack. Let him see the wolf begin to appear. Let him see the monster I could be.

He held my stare for a good three seconds before he dropped his eyes to my lengthening snout. I pulled my lip up, exposing my canines as a reminder of my Alpha status. Snarled at him for good measure, even.

He blinked twice then looked away. Surrendering.

I smirked even as I slid back into my complete human form. "Next time you decide to try to fuck me, champ, just drop to your knees and give the tip a swirl instead. I like a little tongue action, and you're not wolf enough to get a damn thing from me."

My new friend growled but still couldn't meet my stare. Typical. But as much as I liked fucking with shifters who thought they were hot shit, I didn't have the time. My little show would have to be enough to keep the punk in his place.

"Let's get back to business, shall we? My boys and I smelled blood and knew there was something much more our speed than the little lap dance and titty action we had going in the private room." I licked my lips and shot a pointed look at Morris. "We just want to join in on the fun."

The iceman stood quiet for a long period while Morris shook in my hands. The power play between the two wasn't quite what I'd assumed it would be. Iceman was obviously running this show, not the man claiming to be the manager.

Finally, Iceman said, "Let them," before turning to walk away, confirming my suspicions.

"But we don't have enough girls, Caleb," Morris yelled to

the retreating wolf.

"Fucking place is filled with pussy. Find it, and bring them downstairs. I need to deal with a cleanup." And then he disappeared around the corner.

"Hear that, Morris?" Gates leaned forward, practically spitting in the man's face. "Caleb said to find us some pussy. I'm in the mood to get a little rough."

Charlotte

TEN MINUTES AFTER TALL, dark, and scary left, the back door to the changing room opened, and Morris walked in. And he looked pissed.

"I need you dressed for a full-pink show. Pull out your best, these men are important to Amnesia."

I didn't move from my seat, knowing waitresses were never invited to those types of shows. Full pink meant only one thing—anything goes. They were like the private parties but with higher rates and certain guarantees never talked about outside the basement rooms where they were held. And they were a closely guarded secret of the club.

But then Morris pointed at me. "You too, Cherry."

I frowned. "I'm not a performer."

He ran a hand over his greasy hair and scowled. "You are tonight."

My stomach dropped. No. No way was I being bullied into this. I'd never signed on for…whatever happened downstairs.

I stood and grabbed my bag off the bench, ready to get the hell out of there. "Sorry, Morris. But I'm not one of your dancers, and I'm not about to—"

Pain exploded in my jaw.

The unexpected slap stole my breath and caused me to lose my balance. I fell into a wall of metal lockers, sliding down the fronts while my ears rang from the force of the blow. No one had ever hit me like that. I reached up and brushed a knuckle along my lip, not surprised to come away with blood on my fingers. What the hell?

Morris—in a feat of strength and agility that made me jerk away from him—jumped over the bench and bent down so his face was right above mine, his expression terrifying. "You think you're better than the other girls here because you don't dance? It's me who keeps you off the pole, not you. I prefer to keep my stage warm with long, willowy women men can imagine having wrapped around them. Not short, fat girls who probably remind men of their mothers. Now, you will join this party and do whatever it takes to satisfy these customers. You will do as I tell you, Cherry. Because if you make one peep of objection, I'll kill you myself."

He stood to his full height and smoothed his hair off his forehead, practically gloating as I cowered at his feet.

"Tonight, the only time I want your mouth open is when there's a paying customer shoving his dick inside it. Now get up, clean up, and go downstairs. The men are waiting." Morris took a good look around the room. "That goes for you two as well. The damned Feral Breed are here. This night must go perfectly."

As soon as he strode out the back door, I released the choked cry I'd been holding. My face burned and my head ached, but it was my heart I worried about the most. This wasn't supposed to happen. In regular, normal, everyday life, this shit didn't happen. Yet there I was, huddled on the floor with blood dripping down my face, needing to get up so I could go sell myself off.

Reality had taken a damned nose dive, that was for sure.

Star hurried over and knelt beside me, frowning in that pitying sort of way that only made me mad. "It's not so bad,

Cherry. These guys might be a little rougher than normal, but the money's good." She paused, looking almost guilty as she glanced at Porsche. "Should we tell her?"

"No. Don't frighten her any more than she already is." Porsche crouched in front of me and pushed my hair over my shoulders to see where Morris hit me. "You're going to need some deep foundation if you want to hide this."

Fate sealed, it seemed.

I nodded, psyching myself up. My heart pounded in my chest, but the rest of my body was slowly going numb. No churning stomach or fast breathing, no nervous sweating or twitches. Whether I liked it or not, I was about to sell my body to the highest bidder. The words Morris had spit at me hit home in a way nothing else could have. I couldn't run—Morris knew where I lived and that I had a brother. If I didn't do what he wanted, he'd kill me. And he wanted me to sell myself.

"Okay." I grimaced as my lip pulled in a way that hurt more than I'd expected.

Star rubbed her hand down my arm and gave me a sad look. "Wear the white lingerie with the sheer cami over the bra. Maybe if you look virginal, they'll take it easy on you."

I nodded once, too far in my head to say anything else. With a deep breath and a heavy dose of acceptance, I shifted to my knees and said a small prayer for forgiveness. I would do what I had to, whatever I needed to, to make it home. Because the idea of leaving my brother with no one to care for him made me sicker than the thought of selling my body. For the past four years, I'd made every decision in my life with him at the forefront of my mind. Tonight was no different.

But this was it. After this party, after I made it home safely, I'd never step foot inside Amnesia again. There had to be a better way to survive than this.

With as much grace as I could muster, I stood, grabbed my white lingerie set, and took off my clothes.

SEVEN

Rebel

MISSION TIME. I signaled for Numbers to stay on the main floor in case Scab needed backup and headed for the stairway. Gates followed me down and past a handful of unmarked doors. The lights were dim, the walls painted a soft tan, and the floors carpeted in inexpensive commercial Berber. It looked like any other basement, though it reeked of sex, blood, and wolf.

And then we turned the corner, and normal flew out the window.

We entered a large room with couches circling what had to be the entertainment area. Six small stages filled the center space, each with a pole in the middle. All empty for the moment. Most of the couches were already occupied, though, each with two wolf shifters. I could smell them, scent the other wolves and humans they'd been around all day, feel their excitement and arousal from where I stood. My wolf paced and snarled in my mind, fighting against the cacophony of input it was having trouble deciphering. This situation was uncontrollable at best.

"Gentlemen." Morris waved us over to an empty couch, giving me something to focus on other than the dread making my senses heighten. "The ladies will be in shortly, so please allow me to inform you of our procedures. There's a three-thousand-dollar buy-in for each of you. Beyond that, the minimum fees are as follows: five hundred for manual stimulation, one grand for oral, three for vaginal penetration, five for anal, and fifteen will buy you a night in one of the private suites. There is nothing our girls refuse to do, so the full night is your best bet if one of the ladies catches your fancy. Auction-style bidding occurs should a girl earn interest from more than one participant; highest bidder wins any and all disputes. We guarantee a satisfying experience whether you purchase a single option or an entire evening. Our girls are discreet, professional, and very well trained." He gave us a snake-oil smile. "Enjoy your evening."

I glanced at Gates. He shook his head and looked away but not before I saw a flash of disgust cross his face. Fine. I'd be the one making all the moves. I sat back with a sigh and checked out the other bidders. None of the shifters in attendance seemed unusual in any way. Each one looked like a regular John Smith—hard-working, middle-class citizens in the human world. Had they actually been human, they'd probably have wives and families at home. But they were wolves, which meant they didn't want wives; they wanted mates. And mates were harder to come by. They probably spent whatever money they earned in places like this—buying sex instead of searching out someone willing to accommodate their kinks. Quicker, faster, and more direct that way, I assumed.

"Think the girls truly know what they're getting into?" Gates whispered, his icy gaze roaming the crowd just as I'd done moments before. I shrugged and glanced around at the others again. While none of them appeared outwardly hostile, our very natures made us dangerous to humans. Especially when we lost ourselves in sexual acts. This entire situation could go from a night of fun to a horror movie in seconds, which was the last thing we wanted.

"No fucking clue, man. But that animal upstairs had blood on his hands. I don't know a lot of women who'd willingly bleed for us, you know?"

Gates nodded, his face stoic and his eyes constantly scanning the crowd. "So what happens when one of these guys snaps?"

After several minutes of contemplating Gates' words, I signaled to Morris. The sleazy git came running.

"Yes, sir?"

"Tell me something. What happens if my friend here—" I smacked Gates in the chest "—gets a little overexcited?"

"If he needs a little assistance delaying the inevitable, we have Viagra available."

"Fuck no," Gates spat with a rumble.

I coughed to cover my snort. I was never going to let him live that one down. "I'm sorry, no. I meant, what happens if while his cock is out, so are his claws?"

Morris leaned in and lowered his voice. "We have a private medical team that will attend to any occurrences of the claw or teeth variety. The girls are all aware of our dual nature and welcome our animal instincts."

Gates wiped his thumb across his lip, looking like a shifter right on the edge. Playing up his role well. "And if those instincts go a little too far?"

Morris snuck a furtive look around the room and lowered his voice again. "There is a private wooded area behind us. Should we encounter a full loss."

I nodded, fighting my urge to punch the prick in the face. "Shit like that happen often?"

Morris gave me a weak smile, seeming to think about his answer. "Rarely, sir."

"Good to know." I shook the man's hand, even though the last thing I wanted to do was to touch the slimy motherfucker.

"Thank you for your candor."

"You're welcome, sir." Morris shuffled off, back to whatever pit he'd been coughed up out of. Fuck, this was worse than I'd assumed.

I glanced at Gates and dropped my voice so the others in the room couldn't hear. "Full loss?"

He grimaced. "The finger-licker mentioned needing to take care of a disposal."

"Dead humans buried on shifter-owned property. That's enough right there to notify Blaze and call in the Cleaners to close the place, though it doesn't necessarily explain the clawed woman. And the club has their own medical team."

"Which means no hospital trips. So how'd she end up there?"

Questions and more questions, still none with solid answers. I sighed and rubbed my hand over my face. "Unless she chose to leave without the aid of the in-house medical staff. A human may hear werewolf or shifter and picture some kind of fantasy, *Teen Wolf* shit, but the reality may not have been exactly what she dreamed it would be. Either way, our girl most likely got her claw marks because of these parties."

Gates nodded. "Human-shifter sex trade is forbidden by the NALB. We all know it happens, but Blaze would never sanction it because of the threat sex with humans poses to the secret of our breed. Human body disposal on shifter-owned property is also against NALB regulations for similar reasons. We've got them on those two charges, even without proof of who the attacker is."

Still more questions without answers, but at eighty-percent sure about the situation at hand, I was ready to call this mission as over and get the hell out. With my mate, if possible. "Let's go round up the guys and call Blaze. Make it his call as to what to do next."

Before I could leave, before I could even stand, a door on the other side of the room opened. The hair on the back of my neck stood up as I stared at the open doorway, that heavy sense of dread only growing. Within seconds, in walked twelve women. Each beautiful and dressed scantily, but only one caught my eye. Only one stopped my heart and made every nerve in my body fire at once.

Cherry.

My joints burned, and my bones popped with the sudden onset into a shift fueled by rage. I was going to rip Pup apart for not protecting my mate as I'd demanded. I was going to—

"Oh, fuck." Gates grabbed my forearm, his claws sinking in deep and snatching my wolf's attention back from our mate. His voice came out low, deep, and filled with a warning I couldn't ignore. "If you lose control, this will end badly for her."

I furrowed my brow, unable to work out the meaning behind his words over the sound of my wolf snarling in my head. *Mate in danger* looped on repeat in my head, revving my emotions past the point of control. Making me shake and snarl and prepare to battle anyone who dared get between Cherry and me.

Gates gripped me harder, claws going deeper. Slicing the muscles in my arm to hold my attention and leaning over to whisper in my ear. "I've walked this earth longer than you, Reb. I know the look of a shifter who's found his mate. Now sit back and keep your claws to yourself. No one's going to hurt her tonight, I promise you that."

"She's selling herself in this shithole." My voice came out low, more growl to the tone than I'd intended.

Gates looked me in the eye and cocked his head. "Does that matter? Does she lose value in your mind because of her profession?"

"Not a goddamn bit, but I can't watch—"

"Then it's a nonissue." Gates shrugged. "None of these assholes will be buying her tonight. But if you shift, if you get us kicked out, we have no way to protect her. So sit your ass right here on this couch and remember that."

Fuck, even the thought of Cherry being in danger made me want to let my wolf rip through my human façade and drag her off to a quiet den someplace. But Gates was right. If I wanted her safe, I needed to stay close to her. Which meant controlling my instincts and grappling with my wolf to keep my human side at the forefront.

Slowly, watching me the entire time, Gates eased up on my arm. I held still, fighting back my shift, holding myself together through every breath. When I felt sure, felt strong in my ability to stay human, I took a deep breath and nodded to the man I saw as my brother. And then I searched out my mate once more.

Cherry stood across the room on the far right side, her face set in a blank expression, her skin paler than I remembered. The women all smelled both afraid and aroused, the scents changing slightly for each one. But with Cherry, all I smelled was her fear. I could almost taste it, and that wouldn't be good for her. To a group of horny shifters given permission to let out their beasts, a fearful partner would be the ultimate treat. Too sweet to pass up.

Morris waved his hand at a brunette near the front. "The ladies will be given twenty minutes to mingle with the gentlemen, and then we shall—"

"I want the blonde with the big tits on the right. Full evening." A burly wolf two couches over laid a stack of bills on his leg, his eyes on my Cherry. *My mate.* She took a step back, the scent of her fear growing stronger, sweeter. More tempting. Every wolf in the room turned his eyes to her as the rapid beating of her heart pounded an uncontrollable rhythm. Yep, too sweet to pass up. This was going to be a bloodbath, and that blood would mostly come at the ends of my claws.

Morris, oblivious to anything other than that stack of cash, practically purred. "Our policy states the girls must mingle, but I see no reason why we can't bend the rules if you are so inclined," he said, reaching for the money.

"Sixteen thousand."

If Gates hadn't grabbed my arm again and cut right back into the same abused muscles, I'd have ripped his throat out for those two words. Without taking his eyes off Morris, he tilted his head just slightly toward my shoulder. It took my rage-hazed brain a minute to recognize the move as a sign of his submission. The red faded, the beast caged for another moment as I waited for clarity. When he pointedly nodded at the burly wolf bidding on my girl, the haze of fury fully cleared. He'd said none of the others would be buying her; apparently, that meant me as well, seeing as how I couldn't have spoken if I'd wanted to. All that would come out was one long, snarling howl, so he was bidding. My Sergeant-at-Arms was buying my mate to get us both out of the situation. Smart fucking man, that Gates.

"We're going to need to see your payment, sir," Morris said, looking almost nervously at our couch. I nodded to Gates, who pulled a card out of his wallet.

"We have the credit of NALB President Blasius Zenne. You can call him and check. We'll wait." Gates flipped the personalized card toward Morris, whose eyes went wide.

"Yes, well…" Morris stared at the piece of plastic with Blaze's signature on it. He knew what it was. Hell, everyone in that room knew that card gave us carte blanche to get anything we need. A bottomless expense account. And right then, Gates was going to use it to buy a human woman.

Shit, that was ballsy.

With a wave of his hand, Morris gave us the go-ahead. "Bidding is on. To the Feral Breed for sixteen thousand."

"Seventeen." The burly wolf growled and bared his teeth, ignoring Morris' very existence and focusing on Gates.

Cherry visibly shivered, looking between the two men who were bidding to buy their chance into her pussy. My wolf howled and tried to force his way past my mental walls, angry with me for not defending our mate. He wanted to fight the burly wolf to the death, wanted to claw Gates' eyes out and leave them both for dead. But as hard as holding him back had become, I fought to do just that. I needed to keep my human side in control. Cherry's safety depended on it.

"Eighteen." Gates leaned forward, letting go of my arm, probably glaring at the other shifter in that evil way only he could.

"Eighteen-fifty." Burly chuckled, not even glancing at Gates. Such a mistake on his part.

Gates stood and approached the other shifter. His ears visibly perked, something I could tell even from the back, and his walk turned into a smooth, animalistic glide. He was letting his wolf out. I didn't need to see his face to know what the other man was getting a glimpse of. Gates was over four hundred years old and trained in just about every fighting style known to man or beast. He owned the title of pretty boy in our club, but he was also one of the deadliest motherfuckers I'd ever known. If the other shifter was getting a glimpse at Gates' dark side, at the demon within the man, he was seeing his own death on a magazine-worthy face.

"Twenty-five thousand," Gates growled right in Burly's face. The other wolf looked up, trying to glare really, but that anger quickly slid into something more like panic. He trembled something fierce, probably battling with himself over whether to challenge or submit. Not that the latter would happen—no one challenged Gates. Not when he let that beast shine through.

In the end, Burly sat back with a huff, grabbing his money and tucking it back in his pocket. And I—well, I took the first deep breath since the fucker had called out Cherry's price.

Gates visibly shook himself before turning to Cherry, his human face back, his eyes and ears no longer wolflike. The fucker even had a small smile curving his lips. "If you would please accompany my friend and me, I believe we've earned a private suite."

Gates held out his hand for Cherry, giving her enough control to let her make the decision to come with us. Not that it was a real decision—we'd bought her from the club. Still, the illusion was that she had the ability to say no. And she did; she could tell us to fuck off, and we wouldn't hurt her. We wouldn't leave, but we wouldn't hurt her.

Cherry made a choking sound in the back of her throat as her eyes met mine. I tried to keep my face neutral, but it was hard. There was so much fear within her. She was positively panicking. My wolf crashed against my consciousness, trying to break through, to get to his mate. To save her from everything that could possibly make her look at me with that haunted, terrified expression. I hated it, hated every second that she stood there, but I had to hold the beast in check and give her the time she needed to come willingly. She was already scared enough—I couldn't let Gates drag her out of the room and compound it all.

Finally, after several long seconds of holding my gaze, Cherry seemed to find herself once more. The look of panic receded, her face going slack. Expressionless. But at least she placed her hand in the one offered to her. Not mine, but close enough. For now.

"This way." As if he hadn't noticed anything odd about our exchange, Morris exited the room, leading the three of us down the hall to one of the closed doors. "You'll be in here for the night."

He showed us inside with an impatient sort of air, then quickly disappeared, shutting the door behind him. Shutting the three of us into a space made for sex and…other things. The room was relatively simple in its furnishings: bed, couch, small bathroom in one corner…chains hanging from the ceiling.

Shit.

When Cherry noticed the manacles dangling in front of her, she cried out and turned toward the door. "I can't. I've never… I'll have Mr. Morris get your money back. Please."

Gates was the one who grabbed her arm, holding her cautiously as he held my gaze. "What do you mean, you've never?"

She shivered, practically in tears. "I don't…I'm not. I'm just a waitress. This isn't part of what I do."

Just a waitress. I exhaled a huge breath, thankful this wasn't something she normally participated in. Not because of my emotions on the subject, but hers. She'd been so scared this whole time, so panicked and almost out of control; it would have killed me to know she went through that on a regular basis. She wasn't one of the regular girls who traded sex for money at the club, but at least she knew I was a shifter. Morris had said the girls were aware of our dual natures. Knowing she wouldn't run away screaming when I told her about me gave me a little more confidence that I could convince her to be mine.

If I could keep her in that room for longer than a few seconds, which seemed almost unlikely as she inched her way toward the door.

"Cherry." The word slipped past my lips unbidden. She stopped immediately and glanced at me, her heart rate still too high for a human. Her eyes too wide to be feeling any sense of calm. "We're not here to hurt you or to make you do"—I waved at the room—"any of this. You're safe with us. Safe…with me."

But that line seemed hard to accept. She crossed her arms and dropped her gaze to the floor, almost shrinking in on herself. "If that's the case, then why did you buy me?"

My eyes shot to Gates, who stared back at me silently. What to say? I could have lied, could have told her whatever I thought she needed to hear to calm down. I could have deceived her even further than I already had and given her some tale about being good and wanting to save her from those fuckers. Partially true, but not entirely.

And my mate didn't deserve partial anything.

So I shrugged, and I gave her the only truth that mattered. "Because you're meant to be mine."

EIGHT

HE WAS INSANE. Gorgeous and drool-worthy, but obviously not running on all cylinders. Some kind of hot, biker sociopath. Or was it a psychopath? Whatever. I was never going to be seen again.

"…you're meant to be mine."

Bullshit.

"I want to go ho—"

"Did anyone hurt themselves earlier in the evening?" The dark-haired guy interrupted, mister smooth voice and slight accent. And handsome…good lord, was he handsome. His good looks didn't affect me, though. At least not as much as the other one. Blondie captured my attention and wouldn't let go, even if there was something not quite right about him. Dark-haired pretty boy? Not so much. I saw past the chiseled jaw and blue eyes on that one, could tell something scary lurked below the pretty face. Something I wanted nothing to do with.

But I still answered his question.

"How would I know?" I crossed my arms and pressed my back against the door, wanting to run. Needing space and breathing room and… Jesus, there were fucking handcuffs right behind his head.

The dark one held up his hands and took a step away. "Forgive my rudeness. My name is Gates, and I mean you no harm. It's just that we smelled blood and thought someone had been injured. It's unusual to spill blood in a place like this, is it not?"

Smelled blood? This entire night just kept getting weirder. I was done. "What's unusual is to be forced into some kind of prostitution ring instead of being able to go home. What's unusual is the way every hair on my body stood on end when I walked into that room back there. What's unusual is this guy"—I pointed at the blond hottie who seriously needed to stop looking at me like he was before I threw him on the floor and did naughty things to him—"making some kind of ownership claim on me. Blood? Blood could be spilled for any number of reasons, from an accident in the kitchen to a kinky customer paying a willing employee. Blood's not unusual."

The guy smirked—*smirked!* the asshole—and glanced at the blond. "Well then, I do believe I've served my purpose. I think I'll take my leave and see if there's anything else I can find out."

Gates stared at me, waiting, making my knees shake and my hands sweat with the power of his gaze. He needed to quit, to look away. Or I did.

"What?" I finally asked, too jittery to hold still.

Those dark eyebrows jumped up. "You're in front of the door."

"Oh." I jumped out of his way, knocking into the chains hanging from the ceiling and making them rattle. My heart jumped at the sound, and my hand flew to my chest. "Shit."

The blond one grabbed my arm, keeping me still as Gates moved past. His touch set me on fire, his hand on my skin something way more arousing than such a simple hold should be.

"Are you okay?"

Shivers. I closed my eyes as heat and lust burned through me. His deep, smoky voice was deadly, the sound rolling over me in waves of pure sin. It calmed me, scattering my thoughts away from the tension of my situation. Made me want to pull my blond fantasy man toward me so I could feel the warmth of his skin all over mine and taste his words as they left his lips. Nothing mattered—not how we'd come to be in this room together nor his claim on me. The only thing my body cared about was getting as up close and personal with the man who made that sound as quickly as possible.

My eyes popped open at the click of the door closing behind Gates. I was alone…

With the guy who made my heart race and my pussy clench without ever touching me.

Rebel

GOOD GOD, HER SCENT. I wanted to breathe it, taste it, bathe in it. I wanted it all over me, and I wanted my scent all over her. And not just from nuzzling and rubbing myself on her. I wanted my scent buried in her skin, wanted it carried in her blood. The urge to mark her with my bite was stronger than I'd ever imagined, but understandable. I wanted every wolf in the building to know she was mine.

"So, what now?" Her voice came out a little breathy and deep, a layer of heat over the wariness. But the scent of her fear lessened the moment Gates left, replaced by the honeyed notes of her arousal. The fragrance drove my wolf mad with want and sent every ounce of blood in my body south to my already-aching cock. That scent meant she felt the mating pull as I did, experienced the drive to bond as the fates prescribed just as much. She wanted us together, but the tension remained. The fear. She wasn't ready to give in to it yet.

Which meant I needed to calm the fuck down and wait. For her. "We wait until my brothers can figure out a way to get you out of here. Speaking of which, what happened to the man I sent to guard you?"

"The kid? He dropped us off in the changing room and said he'd be outside the door." She shrugged. "He must not have realized there was a second entrance."

"He didn't secure the room first?" I held back the roar building in my chest as she shook her head. I would not scare her again, no matter how mad I grew. None of this was her fault…it was on Pup. Fucking kid would be driving the war wagon for the next month for that particular mistake.

"I'm sorry," I said, reining the rage inside, so as not to scare her. "He should've been more careful with you."

She rolled her eyes then walked farther into the room. Nervous, but not overtly afraid of me, which was good. Without realizing it, she orbited me. Circling, never moving too far away. Staying close. A fact I liked…a lot.

"Do you do this often?" She didn't look at me as she asked the question, but her posture and body language spoke volumes. This was her way of initiating those awkward dating-experience conversations humans felt necessary when beginning a relationship. But our relationship was already mapped out and approved by fate; there was no need for small talk. At least not to me.

"Do what? Rescue beautiful women?" I shot her my best smile when she turned, the one that usually had shewolves dropping their panties and climbing on board. Not my Cherry, though. She wore a small glare on her face, a firm look of irritation. As if she'd heard such things before, as if she couldn't be charmed. But as I waited to figure out what to do next, her heart rate increased. Her eyes stayed locked on mine, the pupils growing wider. Darkening. Filling with lust again. Her breathing picked up speed, and mine followed, matching her rhythm. Already my body was responding to hers, seeking out ways to please her.

I really wanted a chance to please her.

Eventually, she huffed, seeming to brush off all that desire. All that need and want. "You call it rescue. I call it buying yourself a date."

Her eyebrows rose, a challenge offered. I settled against the corner of the bed, my body relaxed, trying to make myself seem safer...more docile. As human as possible, perhaps. More of what she was used to.

"I don't need to buy my dates, and that wasn't what we were doing."

"Sure looked like it from where I stood."

The sudden sadness in her voice beckoned me to comfort her. I approached slowly, my wolf's need to stalk his prey making my footfalls soft and silent. Deliberate. We were the hunter and she the hunted, and she knew it. The closer I moved, the more I could see her reaction. Sense it. Cherry gasped and trembled, inching away from me, though not in fright. There was no fear on the air, no scent of panic. Only her desire. It teased me, made me hungry for her. Made me ache.

I stopped when her back hit the wall, my body barely brushing hers. I liked the feel of her breasts against my chest, of her flesh touching mine. So much so, I inched a bit closer so I could graze my cock against her soft stomach. Prove how much she drove me mad.

Leaning over her, I whispered against her cheek. "I'm not here to buy affection from women who care for my wallet over any other part of me. I'm here because you're in danger. Do you know about the girl who was clawed by some kind of wild animal?"

She licked her lips and brought her hands up to grip my arms. "I…think I heard some talk about it. Cinnamon said the girl worked here, though I never met her."

I growled low in my throat, frustration and desire making it impossible to hold back. Her eyes glazed over as the sound caressed her ears. She sighed, leaning into me more, and I took advantage of our nearness to run my fingers over her skin. Up her arm and around her shoulder, ending with my hand against her neck. Holding her in place. A dominant move.

"Yes, she worked here, which tells me there could be something wrong going on in this place. More wrong than you being paraded in front of a bunch of men"—I fingered the tiny strap of the nearly transparent garment hanging from her shoulders—"wearing only this."

She tilted her head back and looked up at me, her eyes wary once more. Her shoulders growing stiffer. "Waitressing is wrong? Because that's what I do here. I serve drinks." She waved a hand down her body. "All this is window dressing."

"And lovely window dressing it is. But what was going on in that room was more than waitressing."

She dropped her hands from my arms, breaking that physical connection. I nearly whined at the loss of her heat.

"Yeah, well, that's not something I do." She sighed, shaking her head. "If Morris hadn't forced me—"

My snarl shook the room, and I had to clench my hands into fists to hide the claws that appeared at her words. "He forced you? How?"

Her eyebrows puckered, and her lips thinned into a hard line. "I wasn't given a choice. I'm a waitress. I don't even dance. I sure as hell was not prepared to sell myself for the night."

"But Morris made you?"

"He didn't give me a choice." She brushed her hand against the side of her face in an almost unconscious gesture of some sort. Her eyes portrayed a sadness that spoke to something long buried inside of me, something purely human. I wanted to save her, to protect her. To keep all the bad things far away from her. I never wanted to see that sad look in her eyes again.

I slid my fingers around her wrist and slowly pulled her hand away from where it rested against her cheek. That's when I saw the mark, a dark spot on the edge of her jawline nearly hidden under layers of makeup.

"What's this?"

She turned her head away and bit her lip but didn't answer me. I gently moved her chin around and wiped my knuckles against the shadow. As her makeup came off on my skin, the dark spot grew larger and darker. A bruise…a large one.

Someone had hit her.

"Who did this?" I fought to control my voice, to keep the deep, throaty rumble of my growl to a minimum. Inside, the beast who shared my body was going berserk, rushing the bars of the mental cage I kept him in and howling his need to escape. My wolf wanted his turn in control, needed vengeance on whoever harmed his mate, but I fought that instinct. Even though Cherry knew what I was, seeing me shift could easily terrify her, especially if my wolf was out of control when he came through.

Cherry, probably sensing the animal-like fury brewing inside of me, tried to pull away. To move out of the storm's path. But I kept a soft grip on her wrist to keep her near, to hold her close so I could use my fear of scaring her in my battle to control myself. This wasn't about power or seduction; this was about her protection. And though I could already guess who in the club would be coward enough to hit a woman, I needed her answer. I had to hear the words.

"Who, Cherry? Tell me who hit you."

She ducked her head, her hair falling over her face. Trying

to hide. I slid my fingers along her skin and gently tucked the hair behind her ear. Letting her take a moment. Giving her the time she needed to—

"He didn't give me a choice."

The sear of the change flared through my body, burning hotter than ever before. I had to get out of there; I had to get away so I didn't scare her. Had to let my wolf out so he could rip and tear and claw until that fucking bastard lay in pieces on the floor.

I had to kill the bastard who dared to lay a finger on my mate.

"Morris is a dead man."

NINE

Charlotte

HE WAS GOING TO kill Morris, but that thought barely had time to register before a shiver screamed down my spine. Oh lord, that growly thing he did with his voice. I needed him to do it again, do it louder and longer. Preferably while his face was between my legs.

Focus, Charlotte. Murder is bad.

I licked my lips and fought back the desire trying to control my body. "You can't kill him."

His eyes—so pale and wild, filled with a fury I doubted I would ever understand—met mine. "No one touches what's mine."

Even through the cloud of lust I seemed to be floating on, I understood the gravity of his words. I couldn't allow him to think he owned me. I'd already had one man telling me what to do that day; I didn't need another one.

"I'm not yours."

He let out some kind of noise that sounded oddly like a whimper. It tugged at my heart and almost made me want to take back the words that hurt him. Almost.

But he wasn't done yet.

"I want you to be." Warily, moving slowly as if holding himself back, he wrapped his hand around my neck and tugged me closer. "I want you to give me the chance to show you how much you already mean to me."

"But you don't know me." The whispered words felt forced, wrong almost no matter how right they truly were. My heart picked up speed, fluttering in my chest. Oh, his smell, his voice. Everything about him worked like a riptide, pulling me out from shore, teasing me under the waves.

He brushed his lips against my jaw in an almost-there kiss that set my skin on fire. "I just want a chance to make you happy. Is that so wrong?"

I gasped against his mouth and slid my hands under his leather vest, fisting his shirt, pulling him closer. How could I resist? Being around this man made me want to do dirty, dirty things to him…and let him do the same things to me.

But, as with much of my life, money stood in my way. "Is that why you bought me?"

"I bought you to keep from killing any man in that room who would have dared lay a finger on you when you obviously didn't want them to." He licked a trail down my throat and nuzzled under my ear. "Nothing more."

His teeth brushing against my skin broke something inside of me, something wall-like and reserved. Something that had been holding me back.

Screw holding back.

"But what if I wanted more?"

He retreated just enough to meet my gaze. His eyes were darker than before, his pupils so large there was only a small line of light blue around the edges. He made that noise again, the rumble from deep inside him. The sound that called to me in some primal, ancient way. Jesus, how did he do that? I leaned my head against his shirt, pressing my ear to his chest.

Yep, definitely a growl. A deep, dark, animalistic growl that sent shivers racing up and down my spine. And it was such a goddamn turn-on.

"I'll give you anything you want, Cherry." His hands trailed up my arms, brushing the sides of my breasts along the way. Giving and taking all at once. "I'll give you anything you need."

Well, that sounded promising. I backed away, running my fingers along the edge of my panties. "Anything?"

Fire, let's play. Surrendering to my desires was probably a bad decision, one that would certainly come back to bite me in the ass at some point, but I was past caring. I'd never met a man who aroused me the way he did. Every glance, every touch of his skin against mine made me crave him. I wanted his hands, his mouth, his dick. I wanted him to make me come, and then make me come again, over and over until we were both spent and sated. I hadn't had a non-plastic-induced orgasm in almost a year, and he looked like a man who knew how to please a woman.

God, please let him know how to please a woman.

He tracked the movement of my fingers as they ran along the edge of the lace over my hips. Left to right, left to right—those light blue eyes almost glowing as they made the trip once, twice, three times. I paused, giving him a chance to look away, to break his concentration, but he never did. He kept staring, kept making that rumbly growling noise, kept looking like a man about to eat me alive.

Just the thought made me shiver where I stood.

"What is it you desire, beautiful?" he asked, his voice whiskey-rough and full of need. Leading me to admit my truest truth.

"Your mouth."

He had me facedown on the bed before I even registered his movement. I struggled to lift my upper body, but he put one large hand between my shoulders and pushed. *Face down, ass up, that's the way we…*

I shivered and moaned as he rubbed his chin along me, breathing hot air against my covered pussy. "Oh, yes. Please."

"There's no need to beg, my Cherry." With one pull, he ripped my panties off, keeping his face buried against me as he tossed the fabric to the side. I wanted to push back, to rock my hips against him and get this party started, but there was one more little detail distracting me.

"Charlotte," I said on a gasp as he licked a straight line along the side of my opening. How was that simple move so hot?

He paused in mid-stroke. Mid-lick. As if contemplating my word. But then he brought his fingers between my legs, trailing up each side of me, circling my entrance, teasing me into a frenzy of desire. I gripped the sheets, moaning through the first shivers of pleasure sparking between my legs.

"Charlotte?"

I glanced around my arm, eyes meeting his. "My real name's Charlotte. I'm only Cherry when I'm working."

He nodded, accepting the words as if that was a totally normal thing—living a life as a different person in a particular situation. He didn't even ask me anything about my real name, simply kept his eyes on mine as he stuck out his tongue and licked me from clit to crease. I had to fight to keep my eyes from rolling back in my head at how filthy the act seemed, but good lord, did it feel amazing. Again and again, he licked along the same path, grinding his face against me every few strokes. Teasing me into a puddle of desire. Heat pooled in my belly as I watched the debauched way he lapped at me, his entire head moving with the intensity of his tongue. His expression almost rapturous as he tasted every private inch of me.

Breaking away from my sodden flesh, he took a moment to

slide a single fingertip inside of me. To tease me with the most minimalistic touch ever. "Charlotte is a much more fitting name for someone as stunning as you."

And then he thrust his finger all the way in, closed his lips over my clit, and sucked. I cried out, my hands fisting the sheets and my head dropping to the mattress. There was no buildup, no soft start to ease me into the act. There was only his tongue and his lips and the wet heat of his mouth as he attacked. As he bowed my body to his will and demanded I come for him. And I wanted to.

Pleasure ripped through me, making my entire body shake with its intensity. He didn't pause, though, didn't even slow down, just continued his assault on my most delicate parts. I tried to speak, to tell him to stop as my flesh became more sensitive to his mouth, but all I could do was chant "oh yes, oh yes, oh yes" into the mattress.

When he finally released my clit from his lips, he slid two fingers inside. The wet noises my flesh made would have embarrassed me at any other time, but all I wanted was more. More of his mouth, more of his fingers, more of him. And when he twisted his hand and curled his fingers to hit that magic spot that made my toes curl, I damn near screamed.

"You like that?" he murmured, all thick-voiced, bringing his lips back against my clit. The rumble, the feel of the air whispering across my soaking wet skin, and the sensation of his fingers rubbing inside of me had me moaning long and loud.

"That's good, kitten. I'm glad you like it." He licked my clit again then gave it a quick suckle. "I love to do this, to taste you as your pleasure grows. How many times can I make you come before you beg me to stop, I wonder. How long can I suck before those sexy-as-hell legs simply collapse underneath you?"

I moaned again, my legs spreading and my hips tilting toward him almost of their own volition. My body was no longer under my control. Every noise, every action, was completely instinctual and in response to the way he played me. And I only wanted more.

He bit along the fleshy skin surrounding my opening softly, teasingly, before sliding his tongue along the crease between my skin and his fingers. "Does this feel good? Does my tongue make you even wetter? I think it does. I think I could slide another finger inside of you to prove it."

And he did, he slid a third inside, stretching me. Making my pussy ache in absolutely the best way. I released a throaty groan at the fullness, at the way he filled me up with just his hand. He chuckled and once again shifted his hand, this time so he could press his thumb against my ass. I jumped at the sensation, equal parts intrigued and shamed by the contact. That was definitely new.

"What about this, kitten? Would you like me to lick you here as well? Should I tease you a bit first with my tongue before sliding my thumb inside? I could work you from both ends, bring you so much pleasure your entire body would vibrate with the aftershocks. Would you like that? Would you like me to fuck both holes with my hands and tongue?"

He licked slowly, dragging his tongue across my asshole. I fought back the urge to flinch as he dragged his thumb along my crease, allowing myself to enjoy the tingles his touch sent through me.

"That's it, kitten." He pressed his thumb again, harder this time, barely breaching the tight ring. "Just a little more. I can feel you trembling inside. You're so close to coming again, aren't you? I've got you right on the brink. I wonder what it will take to push you over that cliff. I wonder what I can do to make that pretty pussy suck me in."

Fingers deep inside and thumb pumping in and out of my ass, he placed his mouth back around my clit and sucked gently. I was so close, so near the edge. So ready to explode from the inside so he could put me back together again. The tension built low in my gut, a deep need for just a little more, just a tiny bit extra.

And then he growled.

The vibration set off fireworks inside my body, sparking a fuse leading to some kind of full-body shudder I'd never experienced before. The way his lips vibrated against me made me jump and try to claw my way up the bed. But he didn't release me. He followed instead, his hand working harder and faster inside of me as his lips and tongue assaulted my clit. As his thumb pressed deep inside my ass and refused to budge. It was all so much, so much sensation, so much heat, so much—

"There's my girl," he whispered, leading me through the void as I continued to chase the bliss of my orgasm. "There's my kitten. Give me a little more; I want to taste you for days. I want to smell you on my skin. Fuck, what I wouldn't give to dive right back into that sweet pussy and fuck you with my tongue. Would you like that, kitten? Would that make you come harder?"

His mouth once again surrounded my clit, but this time, he closed his jaw as he growled louder than before. The vibrations rocketed me through the need and sent me flying for the third time. I came with a scream at the barest touch of his teeth, my muscles clenching on his fingers and thumb. My body shook while he continued to work me with his hands and mouth, drawing my orgasm out nearly to the point of pain. Time stopped, everything in the world floating away. All that was left was him and me and deep, deep pleasure pounding my body with sensation.

As my muscles relaxed and the overall drowning sensation of my orgasm ebbed, I collapsed facedown on the mattress. He crawled up the length of me, the brush of his clothes on my oversensitive skin forcing one last whole-body shiver. Muscles I didn't know I had were going to ache in the morning, that was for sure.

Once his body completely covered mine, he pulled me against him and rolled to his side. I desperately needed that full-body contact, so I curled into his warmth as he wrapped himself around me. Cuddling in a way that spoke of months or years together, not minutes. We stayed like that for longer than I would have expected, both of us seemingly quiet and content as we lay together.

But then he sighed, and I knew I wasn't going to like what came next.

"I want to take you with me when I leave, kitten. I want to show you how good of a man I can be for you." He kissed my ear before tonguing his way down my neck to nibble on my shoulder, his words only slightly slurred. "I want to make you come like this every day, spend hours with my face buried in that pretty pussy. And then, when I've got you soaking wet and swollen with desire, I want you to ride my cock until I make you scream. Because I will—I'll make you scream my name every single time you let me touch you. I promise you that."

"But I don't even know your name." My words came out slightly rough, my voice scratchy and my mouth dry. I needed to clear my head, to push off the last of the lust clouding my judgment. He was talking about *taking me with him* when he left here. That sounded an awful lot like kidnapping, and I couldn't lose myself in the man just because he could make me come six ways to Sunday.

"Well, damn." He ran his hands along my back, pressing me tighter against him. "My name's Abraham Lynch, though I go by Rebel. I ride with The Feral Breed; we're the protectors of the secret for wolf shifters in North America."

I froze, my back stiff and my brow furrowed. "Shifters?"

His silence didn't calm my nerves one bit. My stomach may have dropped all the way to the floor, but at least my mind was definitely clear again. Oh God, what if he *was* crazy? Wolf shifters...I didn't even know what the hell that meant, but I didn't like the sound of it.

"You weren't told?" Rebel's voice came out quiet, the shock evident in his tone. "Charlotte, did you have any idea what you were walking into tonight?"

"No." I reached for the sheet and covered myself as I sat up, my near-nakedness suddenly leaving me much more vulnerable than before. "I told you, I'm a waitress. The dancers staff the full-pink parties."

His eyes grew wide, and he rolled up onto his knees. "Then why the hell were you there?"

"Morris didn't give me a choice; he told me I had to go."

"Shit." Rebel ran his hands through his hair and let his head drop back, looking stricken and almost fearful.

I clutched the sheet to my chest, my own worry growing as I voiced the question I really didn't want answered. "What's a wolf shifter?"

Rebel dropped his chin and met my gaze. He opened his mouth as if to speak, but instead of words, a huge growl erupted and echoed through the room. I jumped as he spun to put himself between me and the door, which flew open a split second later. Gates leaned into the room, his head tilted down and his eyes on the floor.

"Sorry to interrupt, but we've got a problem."

Rebel's growl cut off, but he stayed between the door and me. "What's going on?"

Gates shook his head. "We can't find Pup. I brought Numbers to keep watch over Cherry."

A tall, wiry man stepped through the door. He glanced at me but quickly averted his eyes when Rebel made a noise close to a snarl. The display shocked me and had me pulling away from the handsome blond in front of me. How could Rebel have this much power over these men, to be able to command obedience without a word spoken? That wasn't quite…normal.

Rebel, suspiciously silent all of a sudden, turned to face me while pulling off his leather vest. Eyes on mine, he then reached behind his head and pulled his shirt by the back of the neck, yanking it over his head. Baring all that toned, hard flesh to my hungry eyes.

God, I was totally hot for this insane beast of a man.

With a wary look in his eyes, Rebel slowly closed the gap between us. "I want you to stay with Numbers." He handed me the shirt, a look of pain crossing his face when I flinched away from his hand. "He'll keep you safe until I figure out what the hell is going on around here."

I took the shirt but didn't respond, unable to speak. Rebel waited, looking as if he wanted to say something but was unable or unwilling to speak the words. The tension grew, the pressure building between us blooming into an atom bomb of anxiety. One I knew could be set off with the slightest wrong move.

But apparently, Rebel didn't have the same worries I did. With a sigh, he finally looked away. Leaving me oddly bereft at the thought of him leaving.

"Let's go." Rebel and Gates headed for the door while Numbers stayed inside the room with his head bowed. "If anything happens to her, I will hold you responsible."

The young man nodded. "I'm on it, boss."

Rebel glanced at me, one hand wrapped around the doorjamb. "I'll be back as soon as I can. Then we can talk. Okay?"

His shirt brushed against my thighs, and my fingers twisted into the soft fabric. Rebel was leaving. He had given me the best orgasms I'd ever experienced, claimed I was his, and yet he was leaving me behind. My heart burned and my eyes watered, panic growing inside of me from the first second he disappeared into the hall.

My reaction took me by surprise. I didn't want him making some ownership claim on me, yet I couldn't stand to think of him no longer beside me. We'd only just met. There was no way I should be feeling this need to stay with him that was making my head pound and my breathing escalate. This was all crazy.

And yet…

"Abraham!"

The word left my lips without effort on my part. I needed him. I didn't know why or how, but I knew I needed him.

He stalked through the door before I finished his name, striding to me in a mere handful of steps. I practically jumped into his arms, pressing my face into his neck and clinging to the leather covering his shoulders. Needing to hang on. Needing him.

Rebel hummed and shushed me while running his hands up and down my back. "It's okay, Charlotte. You're safe, and I'll be back to get you soon. I promise." He pulled back and kissed me, a warm, sweet brush of his lips against mine. Something decidedly clean from such a filthy mouth. "That emptiness in your chest is the mating pull. I feel it, too, but I have to check on my brothers. We'll be back together soon, but I need you to be strong for me. Can you do that?"

I nodded, dropping to the floor to prove I could be strong. "Yeah. Okay."

He pressed his lips to mine once more and trailed a knuckle down the side of my face. "So beautiful."

I closed my eyes for a moment, relishing the feel of his skin against mine. The softness of his touch. But then he was gone. My eyes popped open, my tears building as he once again headed for the door.

"I meant what I said, about wanting to give you a chance to get to know me," he said as he crossed the room, leaving me behind. "Think about it, kitten."

And then he strode out the door.

TEN

Charlotte

DID THAT JUST HAPPEN?

I stood in a cold room in the basement of a strip club wearing only my lover's shirt, my thighs still wet from his mouth on my skin. Oh, and another man standing as if guarding the door.

No, really, did that just happen?

Rebel completely shifted my world off its axis with his mouth and fingers, leaving me vibrating with energy and soaking fucking wet. But he'd left. No warning, no "I'll call you," just a promise to come back and a shirt. Which I was grateful for considering the only other clothing I had to wear was my bra and a pair of wet panties. Gross.

Still, it wasn't as if this Numbers guy didn't know exactly what we'd been doing, but at least I didn't have to walk around with the evidence between my legs.

There was no way to explain how fucked up this night had become.

"Can I go home now?"

Numbers stared, his pale brown, almost amber, eyes locked on mine. "No."

And apparently, that was it. "Okay, then."

The silence grew heavy and awkward as the minutes passed. I paced the length of the dresser, wanting to sit but too uncomfortable to be on the bed that probably still sported my wet spot in front of this stranger. I tugged on the hem of the T-shirt, wishing for a pair of pants or shorts to appear. I had this urge to cover myself, to hide all the skin I so readily showed when I worked. Perhaps because of the way Numbers watched me, his eyes taking in every detail. Analytical and unrelenting, I felt like a science experiment under his microscope. I tried to ignore the way his eyes tracked my every twitch as I continued my walk of shame that led to nowhere. Would this hellish night never end?

I wanted Rebel back beside me. I didn't know him, had only just met him, but I had the distinct impression he shouldn't have left me alone. I felt it, a pressure in my chest, a sensation of something pushing against my heart. Something wasn't right. He should be with me.

I was about to ask where Rebel had gone when a loud roar thundered through the air. Numbers turned toward the door and tilted his head, his focus on the ceiling. His movements were precise and quick, much more aggressive than I normally saw. More animal than man. They made me think of what Rebel had said.

Wolves.

But that didn't make sense. Men who could change into wolves were the stuff of legend, of horror movies and myth. They weren't real, and they especially weren't hanging out in a strip club outside Milwaukee.

When a sharp, short scream broke the silence, Numbers growled.

"Stay here." He gave me a glare then ran out the door.

Freedom...sort of. I sat on the edge of the bed, my legs shaking and my stomach churning. I wanted to leave. I didn't know what was going on in the club, yet I wanted to get away from it. But Rebel had told me to stay put. He said he'd come back for me.

Overhead, something crashed and people shouted, the noise making my decision for me. I wasn't going to be one of those dumb girls in horror movies who stuck around too long and ended up slaughtered by the bad guy. It was time to move.

I swallowed hard and took a deep breath to clear my head. Looking around or thinking about my path out only intensified my desire to run wildly, without plan or purpose. The room acted as a trap. If something popped off in the hallway, I'd have no way out. I needed to go, to find a way up the stairs before anything happened where I only had one way out. My keys were in my purse, which was in the changing room. I only needed to make it up the stairs and down one hallway, and then I could sneak out the employee entrance. My car was parked right outside the door. If I could just make it outside, I could get out of there. Drive home to my brother.

Rebel would have to find me, if he even meant what he said about coming back.

Plan in place, I crept to the door, avoiding those freaky chains along the way. Thank goodness Rebel hadn't tried to lock me up in them. Pretty sure not even his handsome face or hot-as-fuck body could have convinced me to let *that* happen. Being careful not to do anything that might catch the attention of people in the hallway, I pulled open the door and peeked out. All clear. At least for the moment.

Breathless and wary of every single sound I imagined I was making, I hurried up the stairs with my heart pounding in my ears. I kept my footfalls quiet. The stairwell was the worst part of my trip, the area where I couldn't hide should someone come to the top or bottom. I needed to be quick and silent if I was going to get out of there, so I hugged the wall to avoid any squeaky steps, and I kept my weight on my toes. I may have been a good teenager, a well behaved one, but that didn't mean I'd never done anything wrong. I'd just been smart enough to know how not to get caught.

A skill I was putting to good use, apparently.

When I reached the upper landing, I pressed my back against the wall and slunk toward the open doorway to the main floor. The silence ramped up my nerves, sending adrenaline coursing through my veins. A quick glance in either direction confirmed I was alone, thankfully. Two deep breaths, and then another peek around the corner. I could see the changing room door from where I hid in the darkness of the stairwell; I only had twenty feet or so to go. I could do this.

With a deep, stuttering breath, and a mental kick in the ass, I stepped into the hall and strode directly to the changing room. I didn't pause or look around. Didn't falter for a single second. That door was my safety zone, my sanctuary. I only needed to get on the other side of it.

Hands shaking as they turned the doorknob, I slipped inside. I leaned against the door for a moment with my eyes closed, taking two deep breaths to calm my racing heart. *Almost out.*

But it wasn't the time to celebrate. Locker, keys, car—that's all I needed to escape. Freedom was within my grasp if I could just get out that damned door. With one last deep breath, I rushed to my assigned locker and yanked it open.

"You smell like one of those whores."

I spun, my heart practically leaping out of my chest. Caleb sat against the opposite wall, hidden behind a double-high rack of lingerie. He glared at me, his face hard and his freakish eyes practically glowing with rage.

"Hey, Caleb." I swallowed and edged back, pressing my hip against the lockers. "I was just getting my keys so I could head home."

He growled, deep and rough and not at all as enticing as the noise Rebel made. That sound connected the dots floating around in my head. The way Caleb made me nervous, the fight-or-flight response I felt every time Morris came around, how I wanted to run away when I walked into the room in the basement with all those men—something wasn't right about them. The same something that made me wet with desire for Rebel made me terrified of all the others. The growling, the light-colored eyes, and the sharp movements.

My stomach dropped as one word echoed in my mind. Wolves.

Caleb, though, was more focused on me. "You're not going anywhere."

A shiver shot up my spine, and the top of my head tingled. Not now. Not when I was so close. Fighting my instincts so I could face the threat and not show weakness, I turned and opened my locker. Showing him my back. Pretending he didn't scare the shit out of me. Every second lasted longer than the one before, every sound deafening. I nearly cried when my fingers grabbed the leather strap of my purse. Just a few more seconds. Almost done. Then I could get the hell away from this craziness and figure out what to do next.

Once I had my bag over my shoulder and my keys in my hand, I turned around. Caleb's face was mere inches from mine, his body blocking my path to the back door.

"You whored yourself out for him."

I lifted my chin and met his gaze. I put every bit of courage into my glare, even as my insides shook with a sense of terror that made my blood run cold. "I'm going home."

I moved to step past him, but he grabbed my arm and dragged me into the center of the room. His grip turned painful as I struggled against him. I hit, I kicked, I yelled, all to no avail. Caleb wasn't letting me go, and I wasn't strong enough to make him.

"You give me nothing, but those biker wolves show up, and you're spreading your legs." He pulled me against his body and sniffed. "I smell three of them on you. You think they're stronger than me? That any of them could challenge me and win? I'm the Alpha in this club, but you let three of those fuckers touch you?"

With a speed that took me by surprise, he ducked down and slammed his shoulder into my gut, lifting me with ease.

"Caleb...stop!"

"No." He strode across the room and out the employee entrance, running across the near-empty lot as soon as we were outside. When he reached the tree line at the back of the property, he dropped me to my feet and pushed me forward. "Move it, whore. It's time I get what's mine."

ELEVEN

Rebel

I RAN UP THE stairs with Gates on my heels.

"Something you want to talk about, boss?"

I chuffed at him, too blissed out from making my mate happy to care about his sarcastic tone.

"That's what I figured." Gates slowed as we made it to the main room of the club. It was late, well past closing time, and the place was empty. "It'll be sad to see you go, but I'm happy for you. Finding your mate is a cause for celebration."

I froze. The thought of leaving the club, leaving all my brothers behind, was not one I'd had time to absorb just yet. They were practically my pack, the only family I had, and I wasn't ready to say good-bye.

"Let's concentrate on finding Pup before we connect the old ball and chain, yeah?" The words sounded false to my own ears, but Gates seemed to accept them without reserve.

"Sure thing, man."

We came upon the rest of the guys, minus Pup, just outside the main entrance.

"What's going on?" I asked without preamble.

Scab was the first to step up. "I have no idea. The humans

left at closing time with no issues. Gates forced Morris to shut down the party in the basement around the same time. Morris snuck the wolves and women out through a secondary entrance at the back of the building. The only one we lost track of was the big-ass shifter working behind the bar. Otherwise, I think everyone…"

He paused, his nose twitching as he tested the air. Fuck. I was going to reek of Charlotte. Not that I minded, but I didn't feel like listening to the crap any of the crew was about to throw.

"Numbers is downstairs with the last dancer." I glared at Scab, daring him to say a word about what he smelled. He smirked and crossed his arms over his chest, the arrogant little fucker. "I say we circle the building and move inside until we converge on the room where he's holed up. Then we extricate the last human and start a search for Pup. If he's not inside, we can hunt through the woods in wolf form."

Each man yipped in agreement. It'd been a while since our last team hunt, even longer since we'd hunted something as challenging as one of our own. We all loved to run as wolves. Hunting as them was a fucking gift.

"No brother left behind," Gates growled as we broke into two groups—him leading Shadow and me leading Scab.

Closing in on the basement room where I'd stashed Charlotte took longer than I would have expected, as the club contained multiple connected passageways. Every door led to more hallways, every turn left us with more doors. It was a veritable maze of come-scented carpet and furniture. The place might as well have been a whorehouse for all the sex happening in it.

Eventually, we made it to the last rooms to be searched. Scab and I were clearing the kitchen while Gates and Shadow guarded the basement stairs. I made a turn behind the line-prep area into a short hall that led to a walk-in freezer, but then I stopped short. My skin prickled in awareness, and my inner wolf tensed at something he sensed in the air.

"Scab." I paused and sniffed deeper, trying to uncover the disturbing odor under the overwhelming scent of bleach lingering in the hall.

"What's up, bro— What the fuck is that?" Scab took a step back, his lip curling over his teeth instinctually.

So, not just me. Awesome. "No fucking clue. I can't smell past the bleach enough to get a handle on it."

Scab whistled long and loud, alerting Gates and Shadow we'd found something. Within seconds, the two rushed into the kitchen.

"Fuck, what is that?" Gates stopped just behind me. Shadow and Scab moved in as well, the four of us creating a wall of shifter.

"I don't know," I said as I took a step toward the freezer. "But I have a feeling it's behind that door."

We moved as one, closing in on the large metal door. I growled with every step, letting my wolf crawl to the surface to better track the scent. I was sure my face was shifting, becoming more wolflike and less human, but I didn't care. I needed to know what it was about the space that had set my instincts on fire.

When we reached the freezer, I didn't pause or wait for some sort of sign that it was okay to move ahead. There was nothing okay about whatever that scent was. So I yanked on the handle and swung the steel door toward me.

Oh my...

My knees nearly buckled as the scent of blood swamped us, making each man whimper. But it was the sight inside the freezer that immobilized all of us.

Pup hung by his ankles in the center of the freezer. He'd

been sliced open from neck to pelvis, his blood drained and spreading into a sticky red lake on the floor. Numbers was wrapped around him, holding his weight, stanching the blood flow with his own body as best he could.

"Holy fuck."

I wasn't sure which man said it, but I knew we all thought the same thing. There weren't many ways to kill a shifter like us. Sure, you could shoot us in the head, and we'd probably die just as a human would. Otherwise, we healed fast enough to avoid most forms of death our human counterparts fell prey to. But bloodletting…that was one scenario we couldn't escape. Without our blood, we couldn't regenerate. And without regeneration, we died. Plain and simple. Whoever did this to Pup knew exactly what our weak point was.

"He's still alive," Numbers said, his voice weak. "Fucking barkeeper hung him here in his wolf form and left him for dead, but I got him."

"Cut him down." The voice coming out of my mouth didn't even register as my own. My body smoldered from deep within, my wolf in sync with my human mind on our next course of action. Find who did this and kill them. Preferably in a slow and painful manner.

No one went after one of the Feral Breed brothers and got away with it.

Shadow, the only one of us with any medical training, approached first. He stepped carefully into the puddle of thick blood on the floor until he could reach our brothers, leaving nasty voided footprints in the dark red slick. Bending to take Pup's shoulders from Numbers, Shadow grabbed the smaller shifter and lifted him into his arms. The scene struck me hard, the sight of my brothers literally holding one another up. Fighting for each other's lives.

Gates pulled a knife from his pocket and wrapped his hand

around Pup's ankles, his movements slow and careful. "Ready?"

Shadow nodded once, gripping Pup tighter. With one quick slice from Gates, Pup fell free. Numbers stepped out of the way as Pup's legs dropped, nearly falling into Scab, who wrapped an arm around his waist to support the exhausted shifter. The hero of the hour for sure.

When Pup's body became horizontal in Shadow's arms, though, he moaned. We all watched, almost frozen in time as we waited for more. Some sign of life. Something—

And then the blood started flowing.

"Jesus fuck, he's going to bleed out." Gates caught my eye, the last moment we had of stillness before the five of us exploded into frantic movement, everyone talking at once.

"Get him out of the cold!"

"There's a counter over here!"

"He needs blood! Who's got the med kit?"

"It's in my saddlebags." I yanked the keys out of my pocket and tossed them to Scab. "You better run, motherfucker."

Scab took off out of the kitchen as I swept the metal bowls and cooking supplies out of the way. Shadow and Gates placed an unconscious Pup on the stainless-steel counter, stepping over the shit I'd sent to the floor. The three of us working together to keep the young shifter still. But good God, the blood. It was everywhere.

"We're going to lose him," I growled, applying pressure to the wounds closest to his neck. The ones bleeding the most.

"Not today." Gates spread his hands over the slices along Pup's abdomen, pushing down. Holding the shifter together. Scab was back within seconds, our emergency medical supplies in his hands.

"Numbers. Take my place."

Once I was sure Pup's neck wounds were covered, I opened the box and pulled out two large needles connected by medical tubing. Crude, but they'd do. Pup needed a transfusion of shifter blood before his heart stopped beating. That was his best chance for survival.

"No," Gates yelled as I tied a rubber strap around my arm, snatching the tube and needle from my hands. "Let me."

I growled and took a threatening step forward, ready to fight for Pup's life if need be. But Gates just leaned closer and looked me directly in the eyes.

"Your mate may need you. Let me be the donor for Pup. You have better things to do than stand here and watch your blood flow."

"Mate?" Numbers looked at me, his brow pinched. "You found your mate?"

"Yeah." I looked to each man in turn. "Her name's Charlotte. That's who I was with in the basement."

Numbers' eyes grew wide. "Why didn't you tell us she was your mate? Jesus, I left her in that room when I heard Pup scream."

I stiffened, thoughts of Charlotte alone in the room downstairs flooding my brain. My girl was not safe alone.

"Scab and Shadow, go downstairs and grab my mate. I want us all in the same place."

"On it." Scab turned to leave, Shadow on his heels.

"Do not separate." Gates wrapped the rubber strap around his arm and tied it off with the help of his teeth. "If that bartender is still around, be prepared. He's strong and smart. Stick together, and bust your asses to get back up here."

The two shifters nodded then rushed out of the room, leaving Gates and me to care for Pup while Numbers looked on.

I helped Gates with the needles, making sure the blood was flowing from him into Pup before taking a step back. Pup pinked up quickly, the wounds on his chest knitting together slowly from the inside out. He had a long way to go, but things were definitely moving in the right direction. And then there was Numbers.

"What happened in there?" I asked, too pissed he'd left my mate to be thankful he'd saved my brother. And too confused over that to do much more than ask questions.

Numbers shook his head. "Like I said, I heard Pup scream, so I searched him out. When I tracked him to the freezer, all hell broke loose. That bartender went all Tasmanian devil on my ass. Fucker was faster than I thought. I don't know what made him stop, but one second he's all berserker, trying to knock the shelves down on top of me, and the next, he's out the door."

"Where'd he go?" Gates asked.

"No clue. I didn't track him. There's no handle inside the freezer, so I had no way to get Pup out. I figured you'd be around as soon as you realized we were gone." He shrugged, his eyes drawn to our fallen brother. "The shift back to his human form didn't help with the bleeding. I did what I could to keep the kid alive."

"You think the bartender's the man-eater?" I asked, focusing on the mission. On the situation at hand. Not on Charlotte.

Gates shrugged. "Yeah, I do. He's got that crazy nomad vibe about him. And he's certainly more dominant than Morris. It wouldn't surprise me if the bartender is the one running the show while Morris is the face of the operation."

I nodded and stared at Pup, looking for any improvement as a lead weight of regret settled into my gut.

"This is my fault."

Numbers didn't respond, but Gates' head jerked up. I didn't give him a chance to question me.

"I left Pup to take care of my mate, but I never checked in with him to see why he'd left her alone. I was too caught up in—" I waved my hand around, searching for the right words "—lust or mating haze or whatever the fuck that all was. I fucking failed him."

Gates snorted and shook his head. "The mating pull is more than lust, Rebel. It's a connection not easily ignored or severed. If you want to place blame, you should look right at me. I knew Pup failed his assignment, and I had the opportunity to look for him, but I didn't. I chose to clear the club instead. I put the humans in front of my own club brother."

"I'm just glad you two pulled your heads out of your asses and came looking for us." Numbers frowned, but his eyes glinted with mischief. "I was starting to feel like a fucking Popsicle in there."

"Bravest motherfucking Popsicle I've ever seen." I chuckled. "We're a couple of sorry fucks, you know that, Gates?"

"I do." Gates nodded and straightened the tubing a bit. "But at least your sorry ass found his mate. Four hundred years and still no match for me."

I opened my mouth to respond, but Scab and Shadow came bursting into the kitchen.

"The basement's empty, boss."

"Good. As soon as Pup is well enough to travel, we're taking him and the girl to the Fields. Blaze's Cleaners can come back and deal with whatever the fuck is going on here."

"The girl's gone," Shadow said. "The basement's empty, Reb. No humans, no wolves. Nada."

My blood ran cold, and the growl that burst from my lips was one I couldn't hold back. I heard Gates spit a single curse before my wolf exploded in my mind, leaving little of the man behind. I was a roaring, slobbering beast as my body transformed from one being to another. There would be no slow shift, no easing into my wolf form. Hatred fueled my change, and that shit burned deep and fast. Bones and limbs reformed almost instantly until I stood on four paws.

"Rebel." Scab blocked the door. The only way out. The only way to my mate. My growl deepened and my hackles rose as I answered his challenge.

But Scab was no chicken. "I'll stay human until we get outside, and then we'll search as a group, brother. We need to find her and get Pup the fuck out of here."

Without waiting for a sign from me, he moved out from in front of the door, and I took off. My paws padded across the floor, my claws clicking on the tiles. I kept my nose to the ground as I followed Charlotte's trail through the back hallway. When I reached the door to the changing room, I charged through it. The resulting crash echoed in the tiled space as pieces of wood flew in every direction.

There. Her scent was concentrated near a particular locker. It must be hers. But on the air I also smelled her fear and the scent of another wolf. One I recognized. The brawny motherfucker with the blood on his hands. The bartender who'd strung up my Pup like a side of fucking beef.

His scent mixed with Charlotte's and moved across the room to a fire door along the back wall of the building. Scab opened the door for me before I attempted to break through the steel slab. I darted across the parking lot. Scab and Shadow soon followed, the three of us racing through the night in wolf form.

Heading straight for the woods behind the club.

Heading straight for my mate and the man who'd stolen her from me.

TWELVE

Charlotte

STAY CALM, THINK FAST, and don't let them take you anywhere.

The words from the self-defense classes I'd taken ran through my mind. I knew I was breaking the third rule by not fighting harder to stay at the club, but there wasn't much I could have done, really. Caleb had thrown me over his shoulder like a sack of vegetables and carried me right out the door. And when he set me down, well...

It's time I get what's mine.

I shivered and kept moving, too terrified of the rage in his voice and the threat of his words to think through an escape plan. Still, it wasn't as if I was in the middle of nowhere. I could see the highway, hear the traffic on the road on the other side of the woods. There would be witnesses. Forget the fact that the lot was basically empty...someone would notice I was gone. As long as Caleb didn't force me into a car, I was relatively easy to find.

So long as someone knew to look for me.

Doing my best to keep from hyperventilating, I stomped my way through the trees, leaving as much of a trail as possible.

All anyone had to do was pay attention, realize I wasn't where I was supposed to be, and follow my haphazard path through the woods. Sounded easy enough. And Rebel had said he'd be back for me. It was almost a promise. Something to believe in. He would find me.

But then we broke through the tree line and came upon a junked-out sedan parked deep in the shadow of the trees. There was no way anyone could see the car from the road or the back of the club. Beat-up, nondescript, and scary as hell—it had to be Caleb's getaway car. Time to panic.

"Oh, hell no." I pulled against Caleb's hold, punching and biting as he grappled with me. Screaming until my throat felt raw, I continued to fight the hulking man, but Caleb kept pushing me forward. Each slide of my feet on fallen leaves brought me closer to the car, to the vehicle I knew would lead to my death. To the end of the game.

There was no way I was getting into that piece of shit alive.

On a particularly strong pull from Caleb, I used his momentum to leap forward and head-butt him in the chin. It hurt, it definitely hurt, but I accomplished at least part of my goal. He stumbled, releasing my arm from his hold.

"Help! Fire!" I ran back the way we'd come, screaming as loud as I could. My footfalls pounding in my head and my heart racing. But what little lead I had didn't last. Caleb caught up with me before I was halfway back to the parking lot.

"Do not run." He grabbed me by my hair and threw me to the ground with a roar. The force of the hit knocked the wind out of me and made my eyes water. But I wasn't done yet. I clawed at the ground, inching my way across the forest floor, trying to breathe as Caleb started to…change.

"What the hell are you?" His face lengthened into more of a snout than a nose, and dark hair sprouted all over his body. Bones and muscles shifted under skin in a grotesque way, making me gag. I backed away, crab walking until my shoulders hit a tree, unable to stop staring. Caleb kept changing, taking a full minute to go from human to not. To something more animalistic, more shocking. More dangerous.

He changed from a human into a wolf.

"Oh, fuck me running. This can't be happening." I yelped as the beast turned my way, as his eyes met mine. I couldn't back up any farther because of the tree, but that didn't stop me from trying. The bark scraped at my palms and cut into my skin, but I refused to sit still and wait for that thing to—

Oh my God, he's growling.

The wolf stalked closer, his eyes intent on mine, his head lowered. Hunting. I didn't know why his posture made me so certain I was nothing but prey, but I did. I knew it. Felt it with a certainty that seeped deep into my bones. That's exactly how he saw me.

"Easy, buddy." I pressed my back against the tree, racking my brain for something I could do to defend myself against an overgrown dog. "You really don't want to eat me. I can't taste very good."

The animal made a sound in his chest as if he was laughing, which didn't make me feel any better about the possibility of what the wolfman had in mind. His eyes nearly glowed as they met mine, that watery green color fitting in his gray wolf face better than in his human one. Still creepy, just more understandable.

All at once, the Caleb wolf stopped, his head rising and his ears pricked. He sniffed, then growled and turned toward the path we'd come down. Ignoring me for the first time since we'd run into each other in the dressing room.

I wasn't sure whether to relax or start praying.

In the next second, another wolf, this one a bit smaller and lighter in color, rushed through the brush. A group of wolves was called a pack. This fucker was in a pack. But the wolf didn't stop, and it certainly didn't come at me. The thing ran straight at the Caleb wolf, paws practically flying over the path.

Rescue by...wolf?

The two met in the middle of the clearing, teeth bared and growls thundering through the shadows. The animals were a blur of flesh and fur and claws, rolling and biting and growling as each one tried to get the upper hand—or paw—on the other.

Lighter wolf was thicker, smaller in size, but fast. He whipped and spun, jumping over Caleb multiple times to avoid being bit. Caleb was the larger, heavier of the two. He used brute strength to knock the lighter wolf down whenever he could track the faster animal's movements. It seemed a well-matched fight, though—each wolf bringing a different set of skills to the battle. Not that I'd seen many wolves fighting. Or any. Ever.

My world had gone completely off-kilter.

It didn't take long until the blood began to drip, but the lights from the parking lot and road didn't reach into the woods so well, and the animals were moving too fast to determine which wolf was the injured party. But at least one was, and that gave me an idea.

Hoping the wolves were too busy with each other to pay attention to me, I edged away from my tree and began sliding toward the path leading to the bar. I couldn't sit there and watch two dogs fight. Let them kill each other. I needed to get back to the club get the hell out of there.

I stayed down, my butt on the ground, as I continued to leave the wolves behind. When I figured I was far enough away that I wouldn't be noticed, I turned over and crept to my knees. I could crawl down the path, no problem. Icy blue eyes and brown fur stopped me in my tracks, though. And then more gray fur. And black fur, and...

I was surrounded by more wolves. Large, furry, scary wolves. "I am so gonna die."

The wolf closest to me made a noise like a laugh, similar to what the Caleb wolf had done. That sound ignited something within me, something fiery and furious.

I crossed my arms over my chest and glared at the overgrown dog. "You don't have to laugh, you mangy mutt."

The wolf stepped closer, but I held my ground. The thing walked right up to me, his eyes on mine, his head down and his steps slow...

And he sat right next to me.

I froze, sitting up perfectly straight. Every muscle and joint completely locked into place. When I didn't think the moment could get any stranger, the thing leaned into my side. Almost... nudging me to pet him? That couldn't be, though. The animal radiated heat and seemed friendly enough, but I doubted it would stay that way if I did something stupid like put my hand on it or try to run.

But when I didn't relax, the wolf nudged me again, his tail actually wagging in the dirt. Okay, fine. I could try to get more comfortable, but I definitely wasn't petting the damn thing. I mean, it was cold outside and I wasn't exactly dressed for that, so I'd borrow some doggie warmth. But petting...no. Never.

Trying not to make any sudden movements, I settled on my butt and carefully leaned into the wolf at my side. His fur was soft but his body more muscular than I would have imagined, surprisingly so. And he was so warm. I inched closer, still staying far away from the huge teeth I knew were at the front. The two wolves—Caleb and blondie—were still fighting, though it was obvious they were tiring out. There were longer breaks between bouts, stretched out pauses as they each caught their breath. And more blood than ever on the forest floor. Considering how nice the wolf at my side was, I sort of hoped all that red stuff belonged to Caleb.

The wolf at my side rocked forward, almost as if it wanted to join in the fight. I lost my balance a bit and pressed my hands into the dirt to adjust my position. But as I did, something sharp stabbed my palm.

"Ouch," I yelped, turning my hand over to see what I'd done.

Two things happened simultaneously, though—blood ran down the side of my palm from where I'd pressed it into a piece of glass, and the lighter wolf turned my way, his blue eyes boring into mine. Looking right at me for the first time. I knew those eyes, had seen that look earlier in the night.

"Abraham?" The word was a whisper, barely a breath, but the sound was enough to distract blondie—Rebel—from the darker wolf. Caleb took advantage of the distraction, leaping two steps toward Rebel and gripping the smaller wolf's throat in his teeth. It all happened so fast, without a real warning, that it seemed to be over before I'd taken a breath.

But then I screamed, and everyone seemed to move at once. Rebel made a strangled sound as he yanked away from Caleb. A third wolf, this one mottled gray and black, jumped onto Caleb's back with a vicious snarl that sent shivers up my spine. The one sitting next to me—the nice one, as I thought of him—streaked into the fray along with a fourth wolf who came barreling around me. A pack of wolves fighting as one, taking down the threat to one of their own. Caleb had no shot at winning, and Rebel...

Within seconds, the fight moved farther toward the waiting car as two wolves battled with Caleb, leaving Rebel lying in the dirt. Once Caleb was pushed off to the side, the wolf that had been by my side shifted into human form. His very naked human form. I had no idea what had happened to the clothes he'd been wearing earlier in the club, but I recognized him as one of the bikers with Rebel's group. That was the final truth, the final piece of the puzzle fitting into place. The wolf that had run out to save me was actually Rebel. And he was hurt, lying in the dirt, barely breathing. With a naked guy running toward him.

"No!" My scream stopped everything. Wolf and human alike froze as I scrambled my way to Rebel's side. As I curled my body around his and covered as much of him as I could. "I won't let you hurt him."

The man put his hands in the air, shock pretty plain on his face. "I'm not here to hurt him. I'm here to help. I'm Shadow, and I'm the medic of this group. Can you let me near Rebel so I can check him over?"

I shook my head and backed up until I had Rebel nearly wrapped around my hips, my hands in the fur of his neck.

Shadow didn't seem ready to give up, though. "Honey, I know you're scared, but Reb there is like a brother to me. I would never harm him. I just need to make sure he doesn't bleed to death."

I glanced between the two, ready to protect the wolf I knew to be Rebel if need be. But the man crouching in front of me held my gaze, his dark eyes locked on mine in a way that screamed honesty. He didn't even look away when his long, black hair blew across his face. Shadow was a man on a mission, one who wouldn't give up, one who seemed reliable and solid. A man waiting for me to make the right decision. For Rebel.

After a moment of mental deliberation, I slid out of the way and signaled to the medic to move in. I would have to trust someone because there was no way I could figure out what to do with Rebel's injuries without a little help. Hopefully, Shadow was the right choice.

I crawled to the other side of Rebel's prone body as Shadow moved in. "I swear, if you hurt him, I'll kill you with my bare hands."

Shadow chuckled as he inspected Rebel's wounds. "Threatening a defenseless, naked man. Looks like boss man found himself the perfect mate."

"What do you mean, mate?"

Record scratch...stop the music.

Shadow went still, his face going blank as he stared at me. A move I was pretty sure he meant to hide his emotions, but you couldn't work in a gentlemen's club for long without learning to read people. He was surprised, and that thought only made me more curious.

When Shadow finally spoke, his voice was a little softer and a lot less sure. "I think I'll let Reb explain that one to you."

"Bad answer."

Shadow ignored me, focusing in on the wolf at my side. Which meant I was waiting on Rebel to figure out what the hell a mate was and why it was a big deal that he hadn't already told me about it.

When Shadow finished checking Rebel's injuries, he sat back and sighed. "Not nearly as bad as it seemed for Rebel. Are you hurt anywhere? I can smell your blood, but it's faint."

I waved him off. "I'm fine. I just cut my hand."

"Okay. Well, Reb should be able to shift in a few minutes. He needs a little time to heal up first. Scab, wanna make a run back to the club for my clothes and to check on Gates and Pup? I think we're covered here for now." Shadow backed away slowly as one of the other wolves took off for the club, leaving Rebel and me in a relative amount of privacy. One I took full advantage of.

"So that's what you meant when you said 'because you're mine,' huh? It's some kind of animal equivalent of love at first sight? Good luck with that. I'm not really a fairy-tale kind of girl." I wrapped myself around the wolf at my side, hoping to offer him the warmth of my body as he healed. Refusing to think about how much safer I felt with him than I had with anyone else in a long time. Instead, I scratched my nails through his fur and hummed a hymn I remembered my grandmother singing to me when I was a little girl.

And I waited for the man who believed I belonged to him to come back.

THIRTEEN

BLOOD AND FATE WERE powerful motivators.

I woke with a start, clawing my way to my feet. Every muscle hurt, every joint ached, but something told me to get up. Get moving. Get her back to safety.

For a moment, a single second, I couldn't remember who the *her* was. But then I took a breath, and the past few hours roared through my brain in a series of images and sounds. The club, the guys, the bartender, the blood…

My mate.

My growls turned to snarls, the fur along my spine standing on edge. Charlotte needed me. She was in trouble. She was bleeding, and I couldn't—

"Easy, boss."

I spun with a snarl, coming face-to-face with a very calm, collected looking Shadow. Teammate. Not a threat.

But the scent of Charlotte's blood was still on the air, and my wolf wouldn't back down until he found her. Found what had hurt her. Destroyed it.

"He's bleeding again," Charlotte cried, sounding almost panicked.

Mate. Mine.

My wolf edged back, closer to where he sensed her. To where her voice had come from. Needing to feel her touch.

"He's protecting you," Shadow said, staring me down. "You need to calm yourself, Reb. She's okay, just got a little cut on her hand. No one hurt her."

But the smell of Charlotte's blood lingered, and the rage of knowing she'd been injured refused to abate. I crept forward, forcing my brothers to back up, not trusting them. Ready to battle even those I'd always trusted to be sure my mate was safe.

"Rebel," Charlotte whispered, her voice closer. "Stop. Please."

The feel of a hand on my hip sent me reeling. I backed into the touch, needing more, craving it. Charlotte wrapped an arm around my ribs and shushed me softly. Calmed me. Gave me a chance to gain my bearings once more.

And when I did, I nearly fell over.

Pain seared across my throat, the wet, sticky feel of blood in my fur tugging at flesh yet to heal. I wobbled, digging my claws deep to stay upright. Knowing I wouldn't be able to.

"Give him your hand," Shadow called, looking past me.

"What? Why?"

"He needs to know you're okay. Put your injured hand in his face so he can see."

Charlotte moved closer, her body almost supporting the weight of mine. I kept my head between her and Shadow, not willing to back down just yet. But then her hand was in front of my muzzle, and I saw.

Shaking, her fingers slightly curved in as if to protect them, she held her hand out for me to investigate. The scent of blood lingered, but the cut that caused it was no longer open. Shadow was right. She was okay.

A thought that caused the adrenaline high I must have been

on to fade in a single moment.

"And there we go." Shadow rushed closer, catching me and helping me to the ground. "No sense making your injuries worse, boss. Just relax and give your body a few minutes to heal."

I was too busy staring at Charlotte to worry over his words, though. My tail rested against her thigh, and her hands hovered over my fur-covered hip. My angel in the flesh.

"Hi." Her voice sounded rough, the simple word a strain. Dried tear tracks stained her cheeks and dirt darkened her chin, but she was still the most beautiful thing I'd ever seen. I clawed my way closer, desperate for more contact but not wanting to scare her. Closer still, every push making me want to whimper, every inch gained something vital. And then I was there, against her leg, my nose close to her knee. With a deep breath, I raised my head, keeping my eyes on hers, moving as slowly and deliberately as I possibly could. Giving her the chance to push me away. To run. To fear me.

But my mate, my gorgeous, sexy mate, did none of those things. She simply sighed as I placed my head completely in her lap and curled my tail around her hip. And for one moment, for a single breath, I was back in the clouds with my angel.

Just one, though.

"Would you look at that?" Scab laughed, interrupting the quiet around us. "She's made a damn lapdog out of him."

I growled, my claws scraping into the dirt below me as I moved to stand up, but that just made him laugh all the harder.

"All joking aside," Shadow said, placing his hand on my shoulder to hold me down. "I do believe it's time for me to examine you. Let me make sure you're healing properly."

Charlotte stiffened beneath me. "Shouldn't he go to a doctor?"

Scab laughed again. "You mean a vet? Because right now,

darlin', he's stuck in this form."

I chuffed, shooting him a look I hoped was filled with malice. When I got back on my feet, he and I were going to have a little chat. Preferably with our fists.

Shadow, on the other hand, didn't mock Charlotte's fear. He kept his eyes on hers as he moved closer. "Don't worry. I'm well trained in field medicine."

"You look like you're still in high school."

Shadow glanced at me, his normally stoic face sporting what looked like a smile. "Well, I guess that would be about accurate. Except my high school days ended in 1941 when I ran away from home to fight for this country."

"You're over seventy years old? How is that possible?"

He shrugged. "We shifters have a long life expectancy."

"How long?" she asked.

I growled a warning. The responsibility of explaining the details of shifting and shifter life fell on my shoulders. Even if I wasn't the one to tell her the truth, I at least wanted to be in my human form when she learned about me. I couldn't calm her fears or reassure her of my place in her life with only fur and claws.

Shadow nodded once to let me know he understood. "Perhaps it would be best if Reb discussed that with you, being as you're his mate and all."

Charlotte's fingers stopped their soothing circuit along my neck and shoulders. "Everyone seems to know I'm his mate. Why didn't he tell me?"

Her voice lanced my heart. I'd hurt her by not explaining our connection, but I'd run out of time. I wanted to explain to her why I'd left her in that basement room, why I didn't tell her right away about us. I needed her to understand that I thought she knew I was a shifter and, when I realized she didn't, I had no idea how to tell her without scaring her.

I needed my human form.

Fighting the pain still shooting through my neck, I whined and rolled off her lap. Fuck, that was a bad idea, but the need to communicate overrode my self-preservation instincts. I crawled, every step causing more blood to seep from my neck. I didn't go too far, just enough to keep my mate safe from my changing body. I didn't want to accidentally catch her with a claw or a kick as I did what was probably one of the stupidest things I'd ever done in my very long life.

"Not a good idea, boss," Shadow said, watching me with more worry on his face than I cared to analyze.

No shit, I thought. But Charlotte needed human Rebel, and I would give her that. Even if it half killed me.

Cringing against the agony of a shift when my body wasn't ready for it, I focused on letting my bones melt and my muscles transform. Time seemed to freeze, making every pop and creak feel as if it would never end. As if I would stay in that shifter limbo between forms for what little life I'd have left. I ignored that thought, though. Pushing harder, forcing every inch of wolf to adjust into my human form. I suffered through the lengthy, painful process until I was a fully formed mass of skin and bone and muscle once more. Sans fur.

"Abraham." Charlotte's gasp broke through the fuzziness my shift caused. I struggled to my hands and knees, exhausted and battered but desperate to soothe her. Blood dripped down my chest, but I ignored it. Charlotte was my only concern, my only need.

She must have felt similarly. We met in the space between the two of us, bodies immediately fitting together, arms wrapping around one another. Her head landed on my shoulder while I nuzzled into her neck. And then I inhaled, and her scent invaded my body once more. The pain lessened in her hold, and the feel of her skin against mine brought a sense of relief nothing else could have.

Mate. Mine.

Ours.

When the wet heat of her tears dampened the front of my chest, I squeezed her tighter. "It's okay, Charlotte. I'm fine."

My mate, my beautiful, feisty mate, leaned back, wiped away her tears, and smacked my shoulder. Hard. "You were not fine a few minutes ago. I thought that wolf was going to rip your throat out."

"Would've been your fault," Scab said. "There's a reason mated wolves don't ride. She made you lose your focus, and it almost killed you."

A deep snarl ripped through my human form, and I prepared for another shift even as another stream of blood dripped down my sternum. I might not have been in fighting form, but I'd still challenge the fucker for talking to my mate that way. And he knew it. Scab backed up, his head down and his eyes on the ground. Submissive. Smart, but not smart enough.

I was halfway to my knees when Charlotte ran her hands over my chest and leaned so her face was right in front of mine. Those green eyes mesmerized me again, and I froze. Staring. Wanting.

"That's enough out of you," she said, looking more tired than I thought possible. "I think you need some time to heal. Plus, we've got a little talking to do." She glanced over her shoulder at the others. "Does he have someplace to stay, or am I taking him to my house?"

"What about us?" Scab called, sounding like a man in need of a serious ass-kicking.

"Scab," I groaned, wanting so much to knock him down a peg or two for being such an ass to my mate. But I should have known my Charlotte could handle herself.

"You can sleep on the side of the road for all I care. I'm

just worried about one man and one wolf, nothing more." She turned her back on my team, totally shutting them down. "Where are we going?"

Shadow spoke up first, sounding as if he was holding back a chuckle. "We're all staying out at the Roadside Inn. It's just up the expressway."

She nodded. "Fine. Let's go."

"What about the barkeeper?" I asked, not wanting to leave some threat to my mate out of our control.

Charlotte shivered. "You mean Caleb."

Her fear gutted me. As if I couldn't protect her? Not that I'd done such a great job, but I'd try harder. I'd keep her safe.

I pulled her against me, wrapping my arms around her. "Don't worry, kitten. He's not getting anywhere near you again."

"He can't. Fucker's out cold." Scab smirked in a way that made my blood boil. "We can grab some of those kinky handcuffs from downstairs and toss him in the back of the war wagon. I'm sure Blaze will have some sort of plan to rehabilitate him. Numbers and I can bitch-ride back to grab Pup's bike since he can't ride yet."

"Sounds like a plan." I met Charlotte's watery gaze, desperate to get her alone. "You ready to go?"

She nodded, letting me help her to her feet. "Think you can walk back to the club? I need my bag and some clothes, then we can take my car to the hotel."

"Of course," I said, still pissed at Scab for blaming my lapse of attention on Charlotte. And yet a part of me, some niggling traitorous corner of my brain, agreed with him. Because I would happily die over and over again if it meant keeping Charlotte safe. And I would fight my club brothers to make sure they respected her place in my life.

Starting with Scab.

Charlotte

"THANKS, SHADOW. I'LL MAKE sure he takes it easy."

That straitlaced doctor wolfman almost laughed. "Good luck with that. Rebel never really was one for following the rules. But let him know the Cleaners are coming to deal with Caleb, yeah? Our job here should be done within a few hours. We just need to know when we're riding out."

"Will do."

He closed the door with a smile and a nod, leaving me alone in the hallway. I trudged back to Rebel's room, my mind focusing on all the things wrong with this situation. Rebel was a wolf shifter. He was also the leader of this group of other wolf shifters. I was his mate, which still hadn't been completely explained to me. And he would live for a hell of a long time without really aging, like Shadow. Though for how long, I had no idea.

There was so much information I needed from him. How old was he? Where did he live? What did being his mate mean exactly? How did he picture a relationship between us working? Or did he no longer see that as a possibility? Did I see it as a possibility? After everything I'd witnessed, I was still attracted to him, and not in the normal hot-guy-captures-my-attention way. The pull went deeper, felt stronger. Everything about him called to me.

But no matter how strongly I wanted him, I didn't know anything about him. How could he expect me to run off and follow him to wherever he lived? Or would he move to where I lived? Or would we end up riding across the country on a motorcycle with a pack of...well...wolves? And what about my brother, who Rebel still knew nothing about?

Shaking off my frustration, I marched up the stairs and down the hall. I needed to put everything on pause. Rebel and

I could get to know each other on my terms, in my town, and then see where things would go. But until then, there would be no more kissing or licking or sniffing or snuggling or growling. I lost my head when he started growling. Every last thought disappeared at that rumble, and my libido reigned over my actions. Nope. Definitely no growling.

Not yet, at least.

"No growling, no kissing, no sex. Period." I took a deep breath to build myself up to the challenge. I had to put a stop to all of it so we could have serious discussions about shifters and motorcycle clubs and mating. There was no time for anything more, no matter how much I ached for him already.

With my mind made up, I knocked on the door to Rebel's room, ready to tell him exactly what we needed to talk about and how we should proceed.

Until he opened the door wearing nothing but a threadbare towel wrapped around his hips.

"There you are." Water darkened his hair and made him appear older, more dangerous. I swallowed hard and stared, unable to pull my eyes away from his body. The way the muscles in his neck curved to meet his broad shoulders. The way the light hair on his arms and chest shimmered in the overhead lighting. How the water droplets cascaded over the curves and dips of his muscled abs as gravity took them toward the floor.

I wanted to lick every fucking inch of him.

"What's up, kitten?"

His whiskey-rough voice didn't just push me over the edge of reason; it tied me to a hang glider and sent me soaring out past the point of no return and into the land of pure animal instinct. I restrained myself for all of six seconds, which felt like a major accomplishment.

"Oh, what the hell."

FOURTEEN

Rebel

ONE SECOND, I STOOD in the doorway watching Charlotte eye-fuck me, the next, her tongue was in my mouth and her hips were pressing against mine, making my cock practically weep in happiness. Now *that* was how you said *good to see you.*

I kicked the door closed and returned her kiss with fervor, matching her tongue stroke for stroke. Without warning, she ripped herself out of my arms. Before I could say a single word, she yanked the towel from my hips and ran her hands over my thighs.

"Jesus fuck," I hissed, growling when she dropped to her knees. "What are you doing, kitten?"

She grinned up at me, a little demon in her angel eyes. "I'm sucking your dick. What do you think I'm doing?"

Before I could respond, she had her lips wrapped around the head of my cock. The heat, the wet…the sight of her in that position, doing what she was doing. Fuck me, there was nothing better.

And then she sucked. Hard.

I fell back against the wall as my knees nearly buckled,

pleasure shooting from my toes to my fingertips. "Kitten, I…"

She slid a hand up my thigh and over my hip bone as she drew my cock farther into her mouth. I growled long and deep, her touch making my balls draw up tight to my body. The sound only caused her to intensify her actions—more suction, faster head bobs, her hands gripping my ass and pulling me closer. She had me completely at her mercy, and I reveled in it. I let her do exactly as she wanted because it was so good. So fucking perfect. I would happily submit to her every day if it meant she'd suck me off again.

My hips rocked of their own volition, chasing the feeling of more and deeper and harder, my hands fisting in her hair. There was no directing her, though. I held on more for my *own* control than to try to make her do what I wanted. Her style of giving head was fucking phenomenal, and I didn't want to interrupt her. So I let myself get lost in the feel of her mouth— her lips stretching around me, the hot, wet suction, and the flat expanse of her tongue running along the underside. Yeah, I let her do her thing.

"Fuck, kitten. Just like that." Biting my lip, I closed my eyes and gave myself over to the lust rushing through me. Every moan from her caused a shiver, every messy slurp a full-out tremble. I was riding on that delicious knife-edge between coming and not, ready to fall over the edge at any moment.

But it was when she took me all the way in, pressed her fucking nose to my abs and let me slide deeper than I thought she would, that the knife-edge disappeared. I tried to push her off me as my rush to orgasm approached the unable-to-stop phase, but she brushed me off and kept on pulling me in deep. Her style morphed a bit, as if she knew I was getting close, as if she could tell how badly I needed to come. She pulled me almost all the way out of her mouth, cheeks concave from the force of her suction, then flicked her tongue against the head before pulling me back inside. The flicks killed me, sent sparks of something hot and tingly up my spine, and made me want to curl my fucking toes. Three more times she repeated that pattern until I felt the telltale tightening of my balls. Unable to stop, unable to resist another second, I grabbed her head as gently as I could and pumped my hips, fucking her mouth until I finally came in long, hot spurts. She swallowed around me, causing me to groan rough and loud as I crashed through the best orgasm of my fucking existence.

This girl was definitely made for me.

After several moments of savoring the aftermath of Charlotte's epic mouth skills, I found myself sitting on the floor with my back against the wall. She sat between my legs, her head on my chest, her fingers drawing patterns on my arm. The woman had knocked me off my feet…literally.

I pulled her closer and kissed the top of her head. "Not that I'd ever complain, but what the hell got into you?"

She shook with something close to laughter, the sound muffled by the way her face rested against me. "I couldn't help myself. I was all ready to tell you we needed to quit this, but then you answered the door in that towel, and my brain went haywire. I had to have you."

My heart froze when she mentioned quitting, though I was unclear on what the "this" entailed. She couldn't be ready to quit on us; we'd barely even started.

"What were you ready to quit?" I asked, bracing myself for an answer I wouldn't like.

"This. Us…kind of." She pulled back, her eyes serious as they met mine. "There's so much I don't know about you, so much to talk about. But every time I'm around you, all I want to do is get naked. That's not normal."

But awesome. I fought to hold back a smug smile. Apparently, I didn't fight hard enough because Charlotte's serious expression turned angry.

"This isn't funny."

I leaned forward and pressed my lips to hers, just enough to knock the frown off them.

"Of course, it's not funny. But what you're feeling is normal for mates. It's part of why the Rites of Klunzad began." I pulled her in tighter and bent my legs to make her more comfortable, to cradle her. "When the inner wolf of a shifter finds their mate, the two go into a hyperactive attraction state. Every touch—" I ran a finger down her cheek "—every scent—" I pressed my nose into her hair and sniffed "—every taste—" I placed a wet kiss to the corner of her jaw "—entices us to bond through sex. We call it the mating pull or haze or sometimes even the imperative."

She shifted in my arms, leaning her head back to meet my gaze. "And that's what these Rites of Klunzad are?"

"No. The mating *pull* is the reason the ancestors created the Rites. To give the wolf and mate time to bond properly. The two are sequestered for three days while the rest of the pack stands guard over them." I leaned down and nibbled my way from her chin to her ear. "Three days. All alone. With nothing to distract us from giving in to the pull we feel around each other."

She moaned and tilted her head back as I continued my journey down her neck. The taste of her drove me wild, sending all blood back to my cock. Making me need once more. I slid my hand up her T-shirt, only pausing when my fingertips brushed against the lace of her bra. Tracing the edge of it in question. When she didn't protest, when she leaned into my touch as if wanting more, I cupped her breast and kneaded the heavy flesh. She wriggled closer and pulled on my shoulders, a whispered groan escaping her lips as her entire body responded to my touch. The sound drew a rumble out of me, a deep, throaty growl of possession that I couldn't hold back. Her nipple hardened against my palm in response, and her hips rotated against mine. Seeking something more. And fuck, I wanted to give that to her. I wanted to flip her over, to cover her delicious curves with my body, and make her come too many times to count before letting myself fall again. But before I could make my next move, she jerked away and put her hands up between us. Stopping me even as her lust-blown eyes met mine and her chest heaved with every breath.

"I don't have three days to do whatever it is we'd do during these Rites. I have to pick up my brother in a few hours."

Well…okay. Sex on hold for a minute. I blew out a deep breath and focused on her face, forcing my cock to stand down as I felt this was something more important. "You have a brother?"

She nodded, looking almost panicked. "He stays with friends when I have to work late, but I'm going to need to pick him up soon."

"Soon?"

She licked her lips, sagging back into my hold. Relaxing once more. "Yeah, soon."

I flicked my thumb over her nipple and nibbled on her chin. Her eyes locked on mine as I continued my subtle torment to her breast, twisting and massaging in equal measure. A little pleasure followed by a little pain, just enough to keep her on edge.

"How soon, kitten?"

She shivered and gasped on a particularly sharp twist. "I need to pick him up by nine."

I glanced at the alarm clock across the room. "It's not even six yet; we have time."

"But we haven't slept." Her words were breathy and weak, and she continued to writhe in my lap. She wanted this. Wanted me. I grinned and wrapped my arms tighter, abandoning my new favorite toy and pulling her chest against mine.

"If I only get three hours with you today, I sure as hell don't want to spend them sleeping."

I crushed my lips to hers, drawing a long, low moan as I stroked her tongue with mine. Charlotte wrapped her arms around my neck, shifting her legs to straddle me. To push me back against the wall and climb right over top of me. Her body slid down mine in a slow, sensual drop that had me on the edge of my fucking sanity. I knew she'd eventually press herself against my cock, but she took her time. She teased. She awakened every single inch of me with the way she moved. And I broke.

Unable to resist a second more, I yanked her down into my lap, thrusting my hips to press us together where we wanted it most. The moment her soft, wet heat met my cock, I growled. Unable to help myself. Unable to resist.

"Yes, fuck." Charlotte rotated her hips against mine, the pressure both sweet and raw. The tease only growing, becoming harder to resist. The need to slide inside overwhelming. But first, I needed her naked.

"Wait, Charlotte." I bent over her, laying her on her back in front of me. Her legs spread around my shoulders as I pulled them up. "Let's get these jeans off before you hurt something very precious to both of us."

She laughed and her cheeks flushed a soft shade of pink. That color captivated me. My mate was so beautiful, so perfect. I had the sudden urge to climb on top of her and rut to my heart's content, to satisfy my need and my cock while giving her everything I could to satiate her needs. But she deserved better than that. She deserved romance and sweet words, presents and promises. Things I had no experience giving someone.

Things a man like me couldn't offer.

"Where'd you go?" She smiled up at me, but it was no use. I could barely look at her, the weight of my failure suddenly squeezing my chest and making it hard to breathe.

"Rebel?"

I ran my fingers over the waistband of her jeans, no longer ready to remove them. The floor seemed too hard, the carpet too dirty. This wasn't the right place.

"You deserve better than this."

Charlotte cocked her head to the side, her question evident in her eyes. I waved my hand to indicate the shitty hotel room I'd rented. Chipped furniture, an old tube TV that probably didn't even work, and bedding that had definitely seen better days. It was good enough for me, but not my mate. She shouldn't be slumming in some no-name roadside inn. But she simply stared at me, waiting, as if she had no idea what I was talking about.

"This," I murmured, almost growling over the words. "You deserve so much better than this."

She glanced around as if it was her first time seeing the place. And maybe it was. Her entrance hadn't exactly given me much time to offer a tour. I followed her eyes as they took in everything about the room. The dirty walls and cheap bedding made me feel as if I'd somehow failed her again. The dark and dingy bathroom caused my stomach to burn as guilt flooded me. My first real duty as a mate was to take care of her, and I had yet to accomplish that goal. From the time I'd sent her off with Pup, I'd been making mistake after mistake where she was concerned. How I got her to come this far, I had no idea. But there was no way she'd accept such a dump as a place for our first true mating.

But Charlotte tended to surprise me. After taking a quick survey of the room, she shrugged. "It's not the Ritz-Carlton, but I'm not exactly a high-class kind of girl."

"Maybe not, but you're way better than this dump."

With a sigh, she stood and yanked her pants down over her hips, bending to pull her feet through the legs. She wore no panties underneath, not even the scraps of lace she'd had on earlier in the evening. I took in the sight of her as she stood before me. Her curves, her softness, the way her hips flared, how the small T-shirt she wore accentuated the fullness of her breasts—all signs of her womanhood. And all things that spoke to both the man and the wolf inside of me.

"Kitten—"

But my mate spoke right over me. "This so-called dump has a fabulous dirty vibe to it—it makes me want to be especially naughty."

My wolf perked up inside of me, my cock hardening once more at her words. Could she really be okay with *this*?

She didn't try to hide a single inch of herself as she stepped toward me, her eyes locked on mine. "Be naughty with me, Abraham."

Her whispered invitation made my cock twitch and my heart jump in my chest. I could do that. I could throw her down and do all sorts of naughty things to her, with her, for her. I could take care of her needs this way, that was for sure.

I let my eyes travel to the juncture between her legs, gave myself a moment to look as she cocked a hip and gave me a bit of a show. Her bare pussy looked soft and swollen, teased and ready for more. Just seeing that flesh reminded me of her taste and the way she'd yelled my name while I'd loved her with my mouth. I wanted to do it again, taste her again, hear my name on her lips again. Hear it all morning long.

Fuck the dirty room—if it didn't bother Charlotte, I wouldn't let it bother me.

I lifted up on my knees and crawled forward, my hands wrapping around her hips as she pulled her shirt over her head.

When her hair had once again settled along her creamy flesh, I reached and unhooked her bra, never breaking eye contact. Letting my fingers slide over her skin as I dragged the two sides of fabric against one another. The clips released, her breasts almost bouncing as elastic and wire gave way. Fuck me, she was so deliciously curvy and sexy. I couldn't take my hands away, couldn't stop touching every inch of flesh I could reach. She just pulled the white lace down her arms and tossed it to the side, leaning into my touch like a woman who craved more.

I would give her as much as she needed. Always. "You are so beautiful."

She smiled and ran her fingers through my hair, pulling the locks as they slid between her knuckles. The action soothed me, sending me to a different level of arousal. One built around patience and slow-burning anticipation. One I'd never experienced before. I growled with pleasure, a quiet, sustained sound that vibrated through my chest.

"You sound like you're purring."

I nipped at her stomach. "Bite your tongue, kitten. Wolves don't purr."

Her laugh was a treasure, something I wanted to hear much more of. But she pushed me back onto my heels and lowered herself so she could once again straddle my lap. I pulled her closer, nestling my cock in her folds and sighing as the wet heat enveloped me. Home; in her arms with nothing between us was my new home. My absolute favorite place to be.

Movements slow and careful, she kissed me, all soft lips and light flicks of tongue. I followed her lead, letting the kiss meander from teasing to passionate and back, rolling my hips into hers and running my hands along her back. This was something I'd never experienced, the sensation of warmth and intimacy created by the simple act of kissing. And while I wanted to keep kissing her forever, I also wanted to get my cock deep inside her to relieve the ache her nearness caused.

"Kitten." I groaned as she shifted her hips, the proof of her arousal making her slick against me.

She sighed, slowing to an almost stop. "Do you have a condom?"

I held her gaze as I reached behind me, finding my discarded jeans and pulling out my wallet. I handed it to her without reservation. She looked from the black leather square to me and back again.

"I have no secrets," I said, nodding toward the wallet. "You'll find a condom in the pocket behind my license."

She opened the wallet, her movements slow and shaky. I knew the moment she saw the license by the way her lips curled up in a smile.

"You were born January 14th, 1966?" Her eyes traveled over my face, taking in every detail. "You don't look that old."

"I was born January 14th, 1776. I was turned into a shifter in the summer of 1794 during a skirmish over unfair taxation." I pulled the wallet from her hands and retrieved the condom before tossing the leather behind me once more. "And while we shifters have the means to update our identification regularly so we can avoid sticky situations, I've chosen not to yet. I like that my real birthdate and my fake birthdate are so similar."

She blinked twice, her face void of any emotion. "You're over two hundred years old."

"I am."

"And how long will you live?"

"As long as I don't get shot in the head or lose the vast majority of my blood in one go, there's no real set end date. I've met shifters over six hundred years old, and I've seen others die after a mere two hundred years. I'm not entirely sure why, but the unmated wolves tend to die younger than mated ones. And from natural causes. Though Gates creates a huge hole in that theory."

"The pretty one?"

I growled and raised an eyebrow. "You think my club brother is pretty?"

She took the condom from my hand and shifted back along my thighs. With a wink, she tore the foil wrapper open and grabbed my cock. Her touch was soft yet firm as she rolled the latex down my shaft, making me sigh.

"I can understand why some women would find him attractive." Charlotte leaned forward, one hand still on my cock, and gave my earlobe a tug with her teeth. Her teeth on my body made my own gnash together. The urge to bite her, to mark her as my mate, had my entire body shaking with restraint. She needed to know more about me, about wolf shifters, before I could tie her to me that way. But fuck, did I want to.

"Not me, though," she continued, totally yanking me from the spiral of mating bites and claims. "He's nowhere near as handsome as you are. You had me dripping the second you walked into that private room."

"Oh, really?" I reached for her, wanting to squeeze that delectable ass that teased me so brutally, but she wasn't having it. Charlotte smiled wickedly, pushing my shoulders to the floor, knowing exactly what she was doing to me with her filthy words and her refusal to let me touch her. I groaned and lay back willingly, giving up control to my naughty little mate.

"But why does Gates screw with your theory?" Charlotte settled herself against me once more, gripping my cock with one hand and slowly sliding the head over her clit. My eyes stayed locked on hers even as I fought the urge to let them roll into the back of my head. The hot, the wet, the slide of her skin along mine.

"Jesus, kitten. Just put me in you," I groaned as she giggled and continued with her torture. She'd push me right to her entrance then pull me away again. Slip the tip inside, then back away. A perfect goddamned tease.

"C'mon, wolfman. Why does Gates screw up your theory?"

She finally, finally, placed my cock at her entrance and began a slow slide down. Her pussy felt so hot, so soft. It was too much to comprehend. Too much good and tight and fuck. Too much to hold back a groan that came from deep within my soul.

Charlotte lifted almost all the way off then slid down again, settling me deeper inside. Unable to resist, I sat up to suckle her breast, bringing her nipple between my teeth even as I flicked it with my tongue. She gasped and shook, moving her hips faster. Letting me thrust deeper. I pulled back with an obscene popping sound and rolled my hips into hers, matching her rhythm. Almost all the way inside.

But she stopped me with a strong hold on my arms and the tightening of her thighs over my hips. "Tell me."

I moaned and growled, my mind hardly able to focus on her words. "Because the man is over four hundred years old and mateless, yet he lives. No other shifter has lived that long without a mate."

"Hhhmmmm." Her head fell back, her hair tickling my thighs as she finally worked herself all the way down my cock. "So all the rest of the guys you ride with are either younger or mated?"

So deep. So fucking deep. And she still wanted to talk?

"No." I gasped as she clenched her inner muscles. "Fuck, do that again."

She did, and my cock positively rejoiced. I pulled her tight and shivered against her as the pleasure tingled up my spine.

"Ahhh, ffuuucccckkkkkkkk."

"So if Gates—"

"Enough talking." I growled and flipped her onto her back,

angling her hips off the floor. "My brain can't work right when my cock's deep inside you."

"We could always stop," she said, that evil glint back in her eye.

"Is that what you want?" I dropped my forehead to hers and ground against her once, gently, willing my body to pull out of her warmth if she said the words. And praying to every deity known to man and beast that she wouldn't.

She tilted her head back and brought her mouth to mine, placing the sweetest, gentlest kiss in the history of kissing against my lips.

And then she whispered, "Don't stop."

I crushed my lips to hers as my hips began a pounding rhythm. In, pause, rotate, out—deeper and deeper I pushed until there was nothing more I could do from that angle. Not that such a thing would stop me. I pulled her legs up and over my shoulders to change our position, wanting to add a little pressure to her clit as I ground against her. Needing to bury myself inside of her as far as I possibly could without hurting her. Wanting to feel her pussy take me all the way to the base.

She groaned on my first grind, her body quaking under me. So I did it again. And again. She mimicked every thrust, every slide of my flesh against hers. Matching me on every in stroke, and edging forward when I pulled out. We fucked that way until our bodies were covered with sweat and our breaths were just pants against the other's lips. Until we were both reduced to nothing more than the pleasure coursing between us.

"I want to come so bad." She placed her feet against my shoulders and used them for leverage, fucking me as I met her thrusts.

"What do you need?" My words were rushed, my own orgasm building in the pit of my stomach. I had to make her come first, had to feel that slick vise squeezing me from within.

Needing to wring every ounce of pleasure from her body, I licked my thumb and pressed it against her clit, circling in time with our thrusts. She keened and squealed, moving faster, pumping harder. Still not answering me.

"C'mon, kitten. What can I do to make that pretty pussy tremble around me? What do you need? Because I want you to come. I want you to come on my cock so bad."

She tossed her head from side to side, her entire body trembling. "I don't...I don't know."

Remembering how much she liked it when I growled, I pulled one of her legs off my shoulder and guided it down and across my body. With a small tug, I had her on her side and facing away from me. Sliding into position from behind, I continued driving my cock inside, relentlessly rubbing her clit with my thumb. But that wasn't enough; side fucking wouldn't get her there. So I rolled slowly until my back met the floor and she rested almost on my chest, still pumping my hips as hard as I could. And then I growled. Long, deep, and as loud as I dared in the hotel room, I let loose a growl that made the lamps vibrate.

Charlotte froze for about two seconds before practically screaming my name as she came. Her muscles clenched around me, pulling me into the bliss with her as my own orgasm rocked me from my toes to my ears. Every inch of me felt it, every sliver of skin set on fire as the nerve endings screamed their pleasure.

I stayed supine underneath her long after the final wave receded. I liked holding her, loved feeling her weight on me. Loved the sensation of her skin against mine. And she seemed to enjoy my touch as well. The mating bond felt stronger between us as well, the pull toward her increasing. I had to figure out a way to make this work. To keep my club life and her. Because I wasn't ready to give up either just yet.

But eventually, she rolled off of me

"I think I need a doctor," Charlotte groaned.

I jerked to a sitting position. "Why? What'd I do to hurt you?"

She giggled and fell back on the carpet. "Relax. I didn't mean literally. But my God, am I sore."

"Fuck, kitten. Next time, try not to give me a heart attack." Not wanting her to be uncomfortable a moment longer, I picked her up and placed her gently on the bed. Her blond hair looked like silk against the rough cotton sheets, a juxtaposition that could only make me smile. My angel, accepting the worst of me. Perfect.

Unable to stay away, I slid behind her, wrapping myself around her body. "Give me a minute to rest, and I'll make sure you don't think about that soreness for another second."

She chuckled. "What, you can't just keep going? Shouldn't you have insta-boner, like every seventeen-year-old boy out there?"

"I'm a long way from seventeen." I nibbled her ear and ran my nose along her cheek. "Though I think I've gotten better with age."

She sighed and arched her back, pressing that lush ass into the cradle of my hips. "Maybe, but those seventeen-year-olds have a quick recovery time."

I rolled her forward, rutting against her, letting her feel how hard I already was for her. How hard I would always be around her. No matter how much time it'd been since the last time she'd blessed me with a release.

"Those boys are chumps," I said, making sure to growl rough and loud against her neck. "Shifters are quicker."

FIFTEEN

TWO HOURS AND SIX orgasms later, I was thanking every higher power I could think of for shifter recovery times. Or the almost lack thereof.

I pulled a comb through my hair, having just finished showering. Reb was still in the bathroom, his fourth orgasm taking a bit more out of him than the previous ones. Of course, that one happened in a steamy shower while he had to hold me up against the tile wall. Not that he didn't have the strength for it. But the balancing act took a bit of concentration on his part and flexibility on mine. The poor guy was probably exhausted.

I pulled on my jeans, still sans panties, and yanked Reb's T-shirt over my head. I didn't want Julian to realize I was wearing a man's shirt, but it smelled like him. I had a need to keep something of him close to me. When Reb came out of the bathroom, he leaned against the door and watched me. His eyes were dark, his face serious.

"Why are you staring at me?" I finally asked after several tense seconds of silence.

Reb strode across the room, all confidence and sin wrapped up in a pair of light-colored jeans that hung unbuttoned from his hips. The frayed hems brushed the floor with every step, and the worn-out knees looked ready to tear. Yet they clung to him in a way that was almost indecent, every soft, blue inch a testament to the muscles underneath.

"I love these jeans," I whispered as he finally reached me. I ran my fingers along the edge, dipping into the open fly and swiping my knuckle against the head of his dick. He did the growling thing that sounded like a purr and stared into my eyes.

"Charlotte."

I stopped, my hand still resting against the soft denim. I couldn't move, could barely breathe. Something about the tone in his voice and the way he said my name set my fight-or-flight instincts off. Whatever came next wouldn't be good.

Reb ran his hand up my arm to rest against the side of my neck. Holding me. Trapping me. "I want you to come on the road with us. With me."

I licked my lips, my heart pounding too hard to concentrate, making the words I wanted to say a bit hard to find. But there were two on the tip of my tongue.

"I can't."

His face fell then grew hard, his eyes boring into me. "Why not?"

Julian. Think of Julian. "I can't just leave my life behind to jump on the back of your bike."

"Your life? Working at a strip club? Wearing your underthings to attract the attention of men you don't want?"

The world screeched to a stop. I'd been judged for my job before, but I hadn't thought Reb would be one to look down on me. He'd been in the club at a private party. Hell, he'd bought me! And now he wanted to put his nose in the air as if I was the bad one for trying to earn a living and support my brother? No.

I tried to step away from him, but he followed me, herded

me, trapped me against the wall. A move like that would have been welcomed before he'd opened his big mouth. Not so much anymore.

"Reb—"

"Come with me." He nudged my thigh with his knee, forcing my legs apart so he could move closer. "We'll ride with the brothers most of the time, but we can get a house, make a home somewhere. I can keep working to protect the secret, and you can be with me."

My blood roared in my ears, and I clenched my teeth to keep from raising my voice. "Let me go."

Reb furrowed his brow and backed up a step, releasing me. Looking hurt and confused as if he hadn't realized how forceful he'd been. "What's wrong?"

"What's wrong? Tell me something—what would I do if I went with you? Be your biker bitch? Be your mate and nothing else?" I stalked across the room, my ears burning with the rage flaring inside of me. "That's not enough for me, Reb. I'm not someone who's going to wrap my life around yours and hope to be happy about it. I have plans. I have a degree. I work at the club because the money is good, and I need it while I'm taking care of my brother. But he's fifteen. He'll go off to college soon, and then I can go back to working with computers. I can use my brain instead of my ass."

Reb watched me pace for a moment, and then he shrugged. "So we take your brother with us."

I shook my head, wanting so badly to knock some sense into the man. "You're not getting it. I'm not going anywhere. My brother has school, and he needs a stable home life if he has any hope of getting the grades he needs to get into a good college. I'm here, in Milwaukee, for two more years before I can even think of going elsewhere."

The look in his eyes, the hard stare, turned predatory. I

backed away even though he didn't actually scare me. Okay, maybe he did in some ways, but human Reb wouldn't hurt me. I knew that with a truth that had settled deep in my bones.

But he was still part wolf.

Reb moved from one side of the room to the other lightning fast, standing in front of me before I could even blink. The growl in his voice made my heart leap in a very not-scared sort of way, but I had to resist the pull. Sex wouldn't solve this issue.

"What about us?" He pushed my hair over my shoulder and rested his hand beside my neck. "You're my mate, Charlotte. My chosen one. I don't want to be without you."

"And I don't want to give up my entire life for some guy I just met. I need time to get to know you and give my mind the chance to catch up with my lust."

His eyes practically glowed as they met mine, his anguish obvious. But his voice was fierce, imbued with certainty and promise. With anger.

"I have waited over two hundred years for you to come into my life. I have hoped for this day, dreamed about it. But never did I think my mate would deny me."

His words and tone were the verbal equivalent of another slap to the face. As shocking and unwelcome as when Morris had raised his hand to me at the club. But I wouldn't back down. I couldn't... I had to think of Julian and the promises I'd made him.

"Asking for time to get to know you is not denying," I said, trying to stay calm and find the right words to make him understand. To appeal to the human sharing the body with the beast. "It's being reasonable and realistic."

He snarled and twisted, punching a hole in the wall. I flinched but held my ground, my chin up and my back straight. Refusing to let the wolf in him scare me.

"That's not going to help anything."

He closed his eyes and took a deep breath, obviously trying to calm himself. A good sign, I thought. But when he spoke again, his words were almost completely said in a growl.

"You are the mate of a shifter, Charlotte. Realism went out the window the second my wolf chose you."

"And what about the man?" I asked. His confused look told me more than any words could. I didn't want to finish my question, but I needed to. I had to know the answer. "Did the man choose me as well? Or is the human side of you still on the fence?"

Rebel shook his head. "It doesn't matter. You're my chosen female; my wolf would not choose wrongly."

My heart shrank as a feeling of nausea swept over me. He didn't want me. His wolf did, but he didn't. And while I had no experience with wolves or shifters, I knew enough about men to hear the words he wasn't saying. He didn't care about me, didn't worry about the life I'd built or even consider what I might want out of it. He had no feelings for me beyond the lust brought on by some mystical mumbo jumbo. Lesson learned.

Fighting back tears, I grabbed my purse and headed for the door. "When you can stand there and tell me the man has chosen me as much as the wolf has, then we can talk."

"Where are you going?"

"Back where I belong." I opened the door and stepped into the hall with Rebel right behind me. The stairs were at the opposite end, seeming almost a football field away. But I put one foot in front of the other and kept going. Knowing this could be the point of no return.

"Charlotte, stop. You're my mate, the one fated to be mine. You can't just walk away from me."

No return is right. I spun, my chest burning with the rage his words brought out in me. "I am *not yours*! I am my own person, with my own will. Just because your wolf rules you doesn't mean it can rule me. I don't want to ride off with you to some unknown location. I don't want to be left behind while you traipse about with your club brothers and do dangerous things. I don't want to give up everything I am because your wolf decided at some point that I was fit for breeding."

He stood stock-still, his hands clenched into fists and his face wearing a terrifying expression. He was pissed. But that was okay, because I was pissed as well.

I stepped up to him, right under his chin so he had to look down to meet my gaze.

"I am not yours, nor am I your wolf's. And I am not running off with some man I just met, who doesn't truly care about me, on the hope we can get along enough to make a life together. I am human, and humans need time to learn about each other before they make those kinds of commitments." I turned and walked away, pausing as I reached the stairwell to take one more look at the beautiful man who had broken my heart. He hadn't moved. His hands were fisted at his sides, and his mouth hung open. But his eyes said it all. There was no love there, no need—only anger and confusion. And that would never be enough.

"Good-bye, Abraham. Tell your wolf to quit looking for love in strip clubs. Look for something real instead."

SIXTEEN

Rebel

"BOSS?"

I growled, the sound coming without thought or purpose. He needed to leave. She'd come back. Any second and Charlotte would come back through the door she'd disappeared behind.

"We should probably get on the road."

My growl turned to a snarl, and my claws cut through the flesh of my hands. No. Definitely not. I wasn't leaving here or her. She'd be back. We were mates, fated to be together. *She would be back.*

"Rebel." Gates grabbed my arm, a move that earned him a vicious glare from me. "What's going on? Where's Charlotte?"

I didn't answer, couldn't. I stared at the door instead and willed her to come back.

"Are you...Reb, are you all right?"

"What's wrong with him?" Shadow asked, a level of fear in his voice that I noticed but didn't respond to. Gates murmured something too soft for me to hear. Me? I kept staring. Kept waiting. She'd be back. She had to come back.

"Rebel," Shadow said, keeping his voice low. "Pup's bleeding again, and I'm about out of supplies."

Shit. My team, my den. My responsibility. And yet…

"Rebel?" Gates asked, his voice oddly distorted. "What do you want us to do?"

Come on, come on, come on. Come back. Just…come back.

But the door stayed closed, and the men behind me were starting to whisper. Harried voices broke through the haze around my brain, words of pity and incredulousness.

Mate…refused…gone.

Charlotte had left me behind. If it was possible for a heart to actually shatter, I was sure mine had. Charlotte, my one and only mate, had rejected me. I nearly stumbled standing still, the weight of that fact almost knocking me off my feet. She was truly gone.

"Pup needs to get to Merriweather for treatment," Shadow said, almost hissing his words. "We have to get him there now."

Gates sighed. "Okay. You guys go in the war wagon. I'll stay with Rebel—"

"No." The word came out harsher than I'd expected, but it was the right one. Pup—our prospect, one of three "Pups" I had the honor of training—needed help. He needed a level of care we couldn't give him here. My mate had left me, but I would never leave my men behind. I had a team to deal with, men who counted on me to lead them. We needed to get Pup somewhere for healing, and I was going with him.

"Reb?" Gates stared at me, a look of concern in his eyes stronger than any I'd ever seen.

I gave him a single nod, a slight cue to let him know I was okay. "We stay together."

Shadow glanced from Gates to me and back again. "So we go to Merriweather?"

I swallowed back the dread that Charlotte would come back and I wouldn't be there. She wasn't coming back. And I had shit to do.

"Round up the guys. We ride as soon as everyone mounts up."

THE ROOF OF MERRIWEATHER Fields wasn't my usual spot to hang out, but that night, I found myself up there watching the sky go by. It was a cloudless night, though still too hot. The humidity hadn't eased at sunset, and the pressure of it made my chest ache.

That, or the fact that my mate was gone.

Footsteps on the shingles were the only warning I had that someone approached. The fact they'd gotten so close without my noticing irked me. I really was off my game.

"There you are." Gates crawled over the eave and settled on the flat patch of roof beside me. "People were wondering where you went to."

"I'm here."

"I see that."

We sat in silence for several minutes, me searching out constellations and Gates…being Gates. Silent and stoic…until he wasn't.

"Are you going to go after her?"

Direct. To the point. Unable to lie my way out of. "She doesn't want me."

"She's human. They're…fickle."

"She refused to come with me."

Gates grunted. "See? Fickle?"

I hummed, not really believing that particular excuse. Because at the end of the day, the blame rested with me, not her. I should have done more. Should have convinced her that our being together was the right decision. I should have been able to make her stay.

But I'd failed. "I may have ruined my chance."

"And if you did?" Gates leaned back, staring up at the night sky just as I'd been doing. "For close to four hundred years, I've watched these same stars dance across the night stage. All without a mate."

If my chest weren't aching so badly, I probably would have laughed. Instead, I shrugged. "You're a fucking urban legend."

"For more than just my lifespan." Gates grinned before turning serious once more. "Four hundred years without a mate, and I'm still here. And tomorrow, when you wake up, you'll still be here, too."

"But you walk without knowing a mate just as I did…until her." I growled, scratching my claws down the shingles as the reality I'd be living sprawled out before me. "Two days ago, I would have been fine without her. Now…"

I couldn't say it. Couldn't find the words. But Gates wasn't about to let me cut and run.

"Now?" he prompted. And I had to answer. Had to give the man I saw as my best friend an honest view of my situation. I had to say the words.

"Now I know what it is to give your heart to another. I know the pull of your soul finding its perfect half." I closed my eyes for just a moment, letting my wolf howl mournfully in my mind before finishing my thought. "I know that joy, and I lost it."

Gates stayed quiet and still for far longer than I would have thought. Watching me. Probably thinking over my words. The man really was an urban legend—no one had lived as long as he had without a mate. Most had gone crazy or become man-eaters, but not Gates. He was healthy, whole, and fully functioning, just as he'd always been.

He was also apparently curious about what mating was like. "It was that fast?"

"Yep. Bliss and agony within a matter of hours." I sat up, my head aching and my body on edge. "You ever wish you could find your mate?"

A muscle in his cheek twitched, his only tell. The physical equivalent of another man screaming. "Every day. I don't think it's in the cards for me, though. But it is for you."

"Except she refused me."

Gates sat up as well, still watching me with his expressionless stare. And when he spoke, his words were simple. Pure. Impossible. "So you get her back."

As if I hadn't already thought of that. "How? She doesn't want me."

"I don't know, but I have no doubt if anyone can do it, it's you." He stood and wiped off the back of his jeans before heading for the eave once more. "The guys want to leave in the morning. Pup has to stay for treatment, but we're all anxious to get to the denhouse and go back to work. I think you finding your mate has thrown the boys into a frenzy."

"They all wishing for their own? Or thankful not to be stuck where I am?"

He didn't look back, didn't even pause as he tossed out, "I think they're more worried they'll lose their leader."

My gut rolled with that statement. My boys, my team, my family. I could never leave them. Would never want to. But just in case...

"Hey, Gates?"

He paused, halfway over the eave already. "Yeah?"

"You know if I ever left—"

"Which you never will."

I sighed, thinking of Charlotte. Thinking of the joy she'd brought me in such a short time. Thinking of options. "If I ever did, you'd be my choice for president."

"And you know I'd turn that shit down."

"I'd still want it to be you."

Gates huffed a sad sort of laugh. "I'm not the leading type, boss. You think up what you want, and I figure out how to get it done."

I nodded, knowing he was right. Still thinking he was the best option to lead the crews. But leaving was a far-off thought, something almost impossible to comprehend.

"She'll come back," Gates said, a firm sort of resolution in his voice that I certainly didn't feel. He walked away without another word, leaving me to stare up at the night sky once more. Disappearing through the small access door on the other side of the roof. It was then, when I was left alone once more, that I knew exactly how fucked I was in this situation.

"She doesn't know where I live."

SEVENTEEN

Charlotte

I RACED THROUGH THE doors of the office building, clutching my bag and trying not to flat-out run. *Shit, shit, shit,* ten minutes late. That wasn't too bad considering how my morning had gone. But being that it was only my third week working for Valcent Consulting, ten minutes could be the end of my fledgling career. I really needed to get Julian an alarm clock that would simply roll him out of bed for me. Though I'd have to add that to my never-ending list of wants, not needs. And my budget wasn't allowing for a lot of those lately.

Stupid real jobs and their stupid low pay.

Still, as I slid into my chair and hurried through my sign-on process, I knew there was nothing I'd rather be doing. I'd left the gentleman's club behind after that night...the one that had led me to *him*. Not that I'd say his name or even give myself time to think about him. The man who'd given me more pleasure than I'd ever known and who still held a large part of my heart was like Voldemort to me. He who must not be named...ever. It hurt too much.

"Late night?" Michael, the cutey from two cubes over, leaned against the wall of my work space. He was nice with kind eyes and this ridiculously sexy tousled brown hair, and he flirted. *A lot.* But he wasn't—

Nope. Still not thinking his name.

"No, not really." I brought up the customer ticket log while pressing the right sequence of buttons to make sure my phone was on and ready for calls. "I have this little brother who tends to take forever getting ready in the mornings."

"How little?"

"Teenager. And before you go there, yes, I know why his showers take twenty minutes instead of five. I don't need a reminder."

"Ah, teenage rebellion. Always fun." Michael chuckled, but it sounded wrong. There was no bite to it, no growl. And as cute and kind and obviously interested as he was, there was no attraction on my end.

Damn that Voldemort.

"So, I was wondering…"

I cringed, searching for an answer to the sort of question I knew he was about to ask. He'd been dancing around me since my first day, slowly working up the nerve to ask me out, it seemed. And it looked like he'd finally gotten the courage. Shit, I didn't want things to get awkward.

Luckily, the bleat of my phone ringing broke the tension of the moment.

"And the grind begins." I smiled at Michael before sliding my headset over my ears. "Help desk services. This is Charlotte. How can I help you today?"

Michael gave me a head nod and walked away as the man on the phone went on about how his database wasn't querying properly. Probably a broken network connection somewhere; something easy enough to deal with. Way easier than navigating the waters of dating when your heart still belonged to a man you hadn't seen in months.

Stupid, stupid Voldemort.

I entered a new ticket and opened the program so I could take over the guy's machine. Time to concentrate on work. "Okay, let's see if I can get you up and running here."

THAT NIGHT, I PULLED into my driveway a little later than normal. The day had been long, and I'd had to stop at the grocery store for rice so Julian and I could eat something for dinner. I couldn't even think about what we'd do tomorrow. I had less than three dollars left in my pocket and two days left until payday. Not a good situation.

Still better than ass grabs and drink slinging, though.

I was halfway to my porch when a man stepped out of the shadows. One I recognized. One who sent my heart racing in both fear and hope.

"Miss Charlotte." The man named Gates gave me a head nod, his bright blue eyes locked on mine. A chill crept up my spine, a sense of danger. A need to run. But fuck him. This was my home, my brother was inside, and I wasn't running from anything.

I lifted my chin and stared right back. "Is he here?"

Gates cocked his head, such an animal thing to do. "Who?"

Bastard. He knew whom I meant. "I'm not playing games with you."

He stood stoic, watching me, appraising almost. I refused to break that stare, to drop my eyes even a millimeter. He wanted to see how far he could push me? Fine. I wasn't afraid to push right back.

Okay, I was a little afraid. But I wasn't about to let him know that.

Finally, he nodded. "He's not here, nor does he know that

I am."

Well, that wasn't what I'd expected. "So why are you? Here, I mean."

"To give you this." He took a step in my direction, just one. But it was enough. I flinched, and those animal eyes almost lit up. Never run from dogs, right? Shit. I'd screwed up already.

"What is it?"

He handed me an envelope, then stepped back. Giving me room. Giving me a look that said he knew he'd gotten to me at the same time. "What you deserve."

I grasped the envelope between my fingers, looking down at it. Inspecting the writing and the paper. "This isn't from... him."

"Not directly, no. I know he'd want you to have it, though."

"How do you know?"

Gates was silent for a moment, and when he did speak, his voice was softer. Less...growly. "Because he cares for you. Because you're his mate, and that's an unbreakable bond."

I huffed a laugh, my eyes burning with tears. "Yeah, right. Didn't seem so hard to break."

"Maybe not for you, human. But shifters are different. We don't usually recover from a lost mate. It's like a missing limb—something you need and simply can't have. Something you miss no matter how long it's been gone." He brushed past me, nearly bumping me with his shoulder, growling under his breath. "You won't see me again, Miss Charlotte. Me or any of our kind. If you have anything you want to say, any message you'd like me to pass on..."

I stared at the envelope, too confused to know what to do. Too...hurt. But still, there were things I needed to know.

"Is he okay?"

"Okay is not the word I would use."

The fierceness in his voice made me look up, made me

watch him. Made me ask. "What words would you use, then?"

"Angry. Hurt. Heartbroken." Gates shook his head, looking furious. "He lost his mate, and that is a pain that never truly ends."

"His wolf lost his mate."

"They are one and the same, whether you like that or not. Hurt the wolf, hurt the man." He headed for the motorcycle parked in front of my neighbor's house, leaving me behind. "Good luck to you. I hope to see you again."

Why did that almost feel like a warning? "You said you wouldn't be back."

"I won't." Gates mounted the bike, sunglasses covering his eyes and a big, predatory grin on his handsome face. "But maybe you will."

The second he drove off, I hurried inside. Oh God, my heart ached. I'd known him...*him*...barely more than a day, and yet he'd broken me so completely. How could I feel so lonely? So bereft over a man I'd only just met? That wasn't normal. Nothing about him and me was normal.

Hell, I wasn't even sure what normal was anymore.

I set the grocery bag down in the kitchen and took a few deep breaths. This was crazy. All of it—every second of that day and every moment I'd spent thinking about him since. Completely batshit crazy. And yet...

I ran my fingers along the edge of the envelope.

Crazy...but real.

It took me longer than it should have to pull the flap open, to work up the guts to see what it was Gates thought I should have. To accept the fact that a wolf shifter had just handed me something in my front yard.

A sticky note was taped to another slip of paper. A sticky note with words written in a slashy sort of handwriting that didn't fit with today's style of cursive.

We promised this for you, so now it's yours. Good luck in your new endeavors.

The writing matched the outside of the envelope, which meant it wasn't *his*. Maybe Gates had scrawled the note. I pulled the two things apart and unfolded the paper. Money. Well, technically a check. Written out to me in a fancy sort of style that didn't match the note or the envelope. And then I saw the amount.

Twenty-five thousand dollars.

My stomach lurched. That was how much Gates and he had offered to buy a night of my company at the club. My fee for the night, you could say. I'd never given it much thought, never wondered if they'd ever actually paid Morris for my *services*. Services I'd performed gladly and of my own free will later.

Jesus, was he buying me again?

But there was no other note attached, no request for meetings or ways to contact him. Gates had said he wouldn't see me again, so this was it. Money. I'd told *him* I worked at the club to support my brother because desk jobs didn't pay enough. He knew I struggled. What he didn't know was that I'd quit the club after the night we met, that I'd gotten a job in my field, and had begged my way into a payment plan with the Julian's school. A lowly IT associate was apparently far more stable than a waitress at a titty bar, which helped my case with Pendelton's CFO. But money was still tight...too tight. Almost nonexistent most days. And as much as it rankled, as much as I wanted to be able to stand on my own two feet, this check was a godsend. This check was freedom from debt, Julian's tuition through graduation, and a cushion for me in case something went wrong. Like werewolves. Or a nasty flu.

This check was everything I needed to live my life far away from the man who'd written it.

"Char...you here?" Julian slammed the door behind him as

he walked into the house. Typical teenager.

I wiped the tears from my cheeks and cleared my throat, needing to be on my A game for my brother. "I'm in the kitchen."

"Hey," he said when he came through the door. His cane led the way, his unseeing eyes hidden behind dark sunglasses. The scars that traversed his pale skin were almost invisible, but I saw them. I knew they were there. I'd had nightmares about them since the first time I'd seen him in the hospital after the accident.

I saw them, and they only served to remind me of how fragile life was.

I grabbed Julian around the shoulders and hugged him to me, always so surprised at how tall and broad he had become over the past year or so.

"What's up?" he asked, patting my shoulder in that awkward, boy way.

"Nothing. I just…needed a hug."

He finally wrapped an arm around me and squeezed. "Okay. Just…not in front of my friends."

Oh, to be a teenager again. "Never," I promised with a laugh.

He held on for longer than I'd thought he would, but eventually, he escaped my clutches. The kid was practically blushing, probably missing the affection and not knowing how to ask for it. No one wanted to like hugging their sister, but with our parents gone, I was all he had.

"So," he said, looking fifteen kinds of awkward. "What's for dinner? I'm starving."

"You're always starving."

"I'm a growing boy."

I laughed, nudging the check with a single finger. Twenty-five thousand could buy a lot of meals and pay a lot of bills.

Twenty-five thousand was life changing for us.

"Let's go out," I said, grinning at my own idea.

Julian, though, frowned. "We never go out."

"I know, but I have a new job, and we can splurge this one time. I'm not saying let's go all out on some fancy steak dinner, but a couple of burgers at the diner seems reasonable."

He shrugged, trying so hard not to look excited at the prospect and failing miserably. "I have been craving French fries."

"Awesome. We should walk, though. I need to stop at the ATM on the way."

I grabbed the check and my purse, letting the locks on my heart drop…even if only in my own mind.

Thanks, Rebel.

EIGHTEEN

"FERAL BREED FOUR CORNERS, what say ye?"

A shifter other than Jameson stood to answer, causing a bit of a ruckus as other shifters began speculating what happened to the former president. Rumors abounded, everything from death by government agency to a breach of the secret of our existence. Not that it mattered much to me. Nothing really mattered anymore other than my denmates and my bikes.

I sat at the back of the room and ignored the drama, my jaw clenched against the dark mood surrounding me. Three months. I'd left Charlotte behind three months ago, and my anger over the situation only grew hotter and more deadly with each day. She was my mate. In earlier times, that was considered an honor among the humans who knew our secret. Young ladies and men would line up every year to meet with the shifters who protected them, hopeful and excited at the prospect of becoming a mate. A chosen love.

But modern times had forced the shifters into hiding, making us something of myth and legend. No longer was being mated to one an honor. No longer did the human world believe in my breed, in the strength of our bonds, in the fated matings.

Charlotte had proven that with her refusal of me.

And the fissure of pain that caused was never-fucking-ending.

My wolf remained silent, refusing to participate in much since accepting the rejection. Charlotte leaving was a harsh blow to the normally powerful beast within, and I wasn't sure if he would ever recover from the loss. And while the lack of contention between the two sides of my soul—man and beast— should've been a welcomed respite, peace escaped me. Instead, I remained twitchy and uncomfortable in my own skin. Heartbroken and in a pain that refused to take a moment off.

In a word, I was miserable.

A fact that had never been truer than since I arrived at Merriweather Fields for the quarterly meeting. Charlotte lived close, closer than any other time since I'd left Milwaukee three months before. I could feel her, sense the pull between us growing stronger as the distance lessened. And that draw, that deep, eternal need, made me want to rage against the world.

"Feral Breed Great Lakes, what say ye?"

I stood and cracked my neck in an attempt to calm the burning inside of me. "No losses. Membership strong."

Blaze raised an eyebrow at me. "I understand you've found your mate. I am surprised to see you here, Rebel."

Every eye in the room stared, every member quiet as they waited to hear what I had to say. Nosy bastards. Only my crew sat silent and still; only they knew how hard this entire trip was for me.

Biting back the growl building in my chest and doing my very best not to show weakness, I shook my head. "My wolf chose his mate, yes. But it didn't work out."

The gasp around the room came at once, an almost involuntary, synchronized sound. Mate refusal was the stuff of nightmares, of stories told to young shifters to frighten them at night. The dark fairy tales of our world that people heard but didn't truly believe. Rejection of the mating bond wasn't supposed to happen in real life.

Except it did. My wolf and I were proof of it. And that story, my own personal fable, would be told for years to come.

Blaze cleared his throat and shuffled through his papers as his brow furrowed. "I see."

After a pregnant pause that only amped up the tension in the room, Blaze cleared his throat again. "I am sorry for your loss, Rebel. We'll move on. Feral Breed Heartland, what say ye?"

"Sir, we've received a complaint of a missing Omega shewolf."

I really should have cared about the goings-on of my Feral Breed brothers, but I didn't. Couldn't. So I sat down and grabbed my beer, fighting hard not to curl my shoulders inward. That scene was exactly what I'd hoped to avoid—the speculation and rumors as each den heard about poor Rebel what I'd wanted to squash. I already knew what they'd say… President of his own den but not enough wolf to keep a mate. Their jabbering would piss off my denmates and cause friction within the overall club. That sort of attention undermined my authority and created chaos around us all. I didn't want to deal with chaos.

Only Pup, the prospect injured the night I met Charlotte, dared to speak up from my own team. "You're a real idiot, you know that?"

I snarled, unable to stop my lip from curling at the younger shifter. He'd been at Merriweather Fields since we carted his ass back from Milwaukee. It had taken weeks for his strength to return, and then he had to go through extensive physical therapy because of nerve damage in his chest. Very unusual for the normally quick-healing shifters.

While working on his recovery, Pup had started taking lessons with Half Trac on ancient fighting styles under the direction of Gates. The young shifter had grown, both physically and mentally. Where once a strong but lean man had stood, now towered a muscle-bound beast of a man. He would be ready for his own patch and road name soon.

But his mouth was about to get him knocked on his ass.

"What do you know about it?" I downed the last of my beer, trying my hardest to keep from striking out at him.

Pup was clueless, though, it seemed. He leaned forward, his eyes intense as they met mine. "I know I fucked up and put your mate at risk. I know I've been working to make sure I never fail you like that again. And being almost two hundred years younger than you, I know Charlotte made the right decision by walking away."

I grabbed him by the back of the shirt and dragged his ass out into the hall, attracting the attention of the shifters around us. Inside, my wolf was ready to tear apart the younger Anbizen, but I had to be a leader first. I had to figure out why the guy was suddenly talking smack. Then I could kick his ass for opening his mouth.

Once in the hall and away from prying eyes, I shoved him hard. Almost knocking him off his feet. "Want to try that again, fucker?"

"I'm not saying you don't deserve a mate." He huffed a laugh and leaned a shoulder against the wall, the picture of ease as my wolf dreamed of ripping his throat out. "But you handled finding her all wrong. You asked her to make a commitment to you, to your way of life, without discussing what mating truly means. And you never gave her a chance to tell you what she needed to feel comfortable with bringing you into her life. I think you should've given her what she asked for instead of walking away."

My chest ached, nearly imploding at the memory of those last few minutes with Charlotte. But my rage burned hotter. "And what, you're some kind of expert on women all of a sudden?"

"Not all of a sudden." Pup took a deep breath, and he looked me right in the eyes. Giving me his honesty. "I fucked up that day at the club, and I promised myself I would never let that happen again. I would never let another mate get hurt while on my watch."

I glared back at him as his words swirled and coalesced. As they painted a picture I hadn't seen before. As they made sense.

"You've been keeping an eye on her."

Pup nodded, looking positively fierce. "I will never fail another mate of my brothers again."

I sat back, unable to come up with a response. While I'd been burying my pain on my bike all over southeastern Michigan, Pup had been making sure my mate was safe. A job that should have rested on my shoulders. And if that wasn't a thought that made my balls practically crawl back into my body, I didn't know what was.

"I don't know what to do," I admitted, the words barely more than a whisper. "She walked away from me."

"No, she asked you for time. That's not the same thing." Pup sighed and leaned in so we could keep our conversation relatively quiet. "I understand how things were done in the past, and I have the utmost respect for the traditions, but life is different now. Women are different. They don't want to be dragged about by the hair, and they don't need a man to come riding up on a white horse to rescue them. They want to choose the path their life follows. Charlotte is an intelligent woman who worked hard for a degree she didn't get to use. That had to sting a bit. Plus she's independent and resourceful. Becoming your little beck-and-call girl would never be enough for her.

But if you took the time to get to know her, learn her wants and her needs, and gave her the chance to choose the direction of her life, she'd probably come around."

"Probably?"

He shrugged. "Women are known to change their minds, but my guess is she'd follow you anywhere if you'd only let her lead."

I shook my head. "That doesn't make sense."

"Sure it does." He grinned. "To a woman."

PUP'S WORDS ATE AT me through the remainder of the meetings. As the moon rose and shifters moved on to other areas of the Fields to relax with their brethren, I sat on my barstool in the meeting hall and mulled over Pup's advice. Or his not-so-much advice. His warning?

"You look like a man with a lot on his mind." Blaze pulled up the barstool across from me and sat down. The fact I hadn't heard him approach spoke to how deep in my thoughts I'd been. And how much I probably needed to talk to a man like Blasius Zenne.

"I guess I kind of am."

We sat in silence for several minutes. My mind jumped from Charlotte to my club and back again, running the gamut from the good to the bad. There was no answer in sight, no way to feed both with the care they needed, and no certainty of a future with either one at this point. I was about to throw my beer bottle across the room when Blaze said five words that completely refocused my mind.

"Tell me about your mate."

Not a question or an option in his statement. Typical Blaze, demanding the most important information. And so I told him.

Everything. Meeting Charlotte, the mistakes at the club, the fight at the hotel room. The gut-wrenching agony of watching her walk away from me. For the first time, I laid every detail out on the table about the day I'd found my mate. And when I was done, when my word vomit ended and I finally found the guts to look up into Blaze's eyes, I knew I was in trouble.

"You realize you have a major problem with your wolf."

Out of everything the man could've said I had a problem with, my wolf was not what I'd expected. "Well, no. I mean, he's been a bit quiet, but—"

"Your wolf is meant to be a part of you, an extension of your soul. Seeing him as a force you must do daily battle with is not normal. You can never have peace if you choose to fight him every step of your journey together."

I hadn't thought things could get worse, but apparently, I'd been wrong. Something not normal with my wolf? An imbalance between wolf and man turned shifters into nomads and man-eaters. Would I one day go from the hunter to the hunted? The thought of my own brothers chasing me down and destroying me to keep me from putting the breed in danger sickened me and left a cold sweat across my skin.

I licked my suddenly dry lips and asked the one question I couldn't bear to leave unanswered.

"Does this mean I need to be destroyed, sir?"

Blaze watched me with those intense blue eyes, waiting until I broke the stare before speaking.

"No. Not yet, at least." He sighed and rested one elbow on the table. "Do you know what most man-eaters have in common, Rebel?"

I shook my head.

"They are packless—nomads. Wolves who go down that dark path are usually either Borzohn shifters who were kicked out of their family pack at a young age or Anbizen shifters who were not folded into a pack upon their turning. They are the orphans of our breed, the rejected. It's one of the reasons the Feral Breed club began. To give our stronger wolves a place to go as available territory grew scarce. Look at your own club. Forty-two wolves, all willful enough to be Alphas of their own pack, but having only a few Midwestern states to roam. Without the club, most of those men and women would be killed off in challenges for pack positions or disputes over hunting grounds. We've seen it numerous times through the centuries."

My stomach sank. "I wasn't folded into a pack when I was turned."

"No, but you are one of the Feral Breed: a strong and loyal member to our brotherhood. You have found your pack, as dysfunctional as it is. You are much like your Gates, who defies all history of wolf lore and continues whole and healthy past the four-hundred-year mark without his mate. He sees your club as his pack, and therefore, remains happy in a family unit. As does Jameson from Four Corners and Throttle from Hollywood—all well past the age when most unmated wolves pass on, and yet they thrive in this pack-like club. Just as you do. And now, you have found your mate, which should bring much happiness to you and your slightly estranged wolf."

"My wolf found his mate."

Blaze glared, his wolf side showing in his eyes and making me tense in anticipation of a fight. "You and your wolf are the same being. Unlike what the popular myth claims, becoming an Anbizen does not force the wolf into your soul. It joins the natural wolf instincts with the human instincts buried deep under a millennium of social conditioning. Few survive the transition because they're not strong enough, and the ones who do tend to be more aggressive than their Borzohn cousins. But that doesn't mean the wolf isn't as much a part of the Anbizen soul as it is the Borzohn. The wolf doesn't exist without you, he doesn't emote individually, and he doesn't act with autonomy. He *is you*. Just the baser instincts inside of you."

My wolf was me, which meant… "When my wolf mated—"

"You found your soul mate. No more, no less. Your wolf side happened to be smart enough to realize who she was. If only your human side could stop fighting against the mating pull." Blaze smirked as he stood. "You live up to your road name, Abraham Lynch. A rebel to the very core, you refuse to allow anyone to claim dominion over you. Even the one woman made to be yours. Perhaps it's time to stop rebelling, young one."

He headed for the door with his back straight and his head up, the epitome of strength and confidence. Something I envied. I'd been walking around like a kicked puppy because I was too afraid to go after what I wanted. Too afraid to lose what I saw as something I needed.

But before he could leave, I had to know the answer to one more thing. "What do I do about my mate?"

Blaze paused, the tenor of his voice infused with the power of his wolf. "You woo her, of course. This is not the age you were whelped in, pup. A woman no longer needs a man in her life to survive. If you want her to accept your suit, you'd better begin acting as if you understand a modern woman. You have interrupted your Klunzad period by being ignorant and dismissive of her needs. Fix it."

"If I fix it, I'll have to leave the Breed."

Blaze finally turned, his face drawn and his eyes dark. "No mated shifters ride, not because of some unspoken rule, but because they choose to settle into a pack. If you and your mate can come to an agreement, you will be welcomed within the Feral Breed. We have no restrictions on who can attempt to gain entry, and we need every member we have and more to keep our packs, our Omegas, and our members safe. You'd be wise to remember that, Den President Lynch."

He walked out of the hall with a growl, leaving me in a cloud of confusion. My wolf was me. My mate was ours. There wouldn't be another chance. Charlotte was human—I wasn't, hadn't been since my turning. Maybe it was time to embrace that knowledge, to accept the duality of my wolf and man and give them both what they wanted. Time to stop fighting and start learning.

To end the rebellion.

NINETEEN

Charlotte

"JULIAN! You're going to be late for school if you don't move it."

"Hold your horses, Char. I'm just tying my shoes."

Julian clomped down the stairs, his backpack thrown over his arm. Dark glasses covered his hazel eyes, and his dark-blond hair hung across his forehead like all the other boys his age. He looked like some sort of teenage rock star, only without the expensive labels on his clothes. I'd be so glad when he grew out of the mimic-the-pop-culture-icon phase.

Someday.

With a sigh and a shake of my head, I handed him his lunch and turned him toward the door.

"Call me as soon as you get to Bobby's, okay? I'll be home all night, so I can come get you if you don't want to stay. And don't get into any trouble." I bit my lip and tugged on the sleeve of his shirt, trying hard not to cling. And failing. "Maybe you boys should stay here this time."

"Okay, okay. I know the rules. No drinking, no smoking, no girls, and don't ever walk into a strip club. I've got it. This isn't the first time I've spent the night at Bobby's. We're just going to play some games and eat shitty pizza. Chill out already."

Sometimes it was really easy to tell he wasn't a kid anymore, like when I had to reach up to smack the back of his head. "When'd you turn into such a smartass?"

"When you quit working at Amnesia and started toiling behind a computer screen all day. You're seriously cramping my style, sis. I'm not a little kid anymore. I can hang out with my friends without you worrying over every little thing."

My sigh couldn't have been any bigger. He was right. Ever since I'd walked away from Reb and the club, I'd been a major pain in Julian's ass. Always checking up on him, worrying whenever he left the house without me, tracking him down at all times of the day. I needed to ease up, but knowing there were men who shifted into animal forms kind of freaked me out. Not that I'd told Julian that particular little nugget.

"Fine, fine, fine, I'll back off. Just text me every hour or so, please? I promise not to call if you let me know you're okay."

"Fine. I'll text. But don't send me any schmoopy messages. I've got a rep to protect." He gave me a quick kiss on the cheek and grabbed his long cane from its storage spot by the closet. He was in full running mode until he opened the front door. The lack of heavy footsteps and the absence of a door slamming behind him told me immediately that something was wrong.

"Julian?"

"Hello. Is…Charlotte home?"

That voice. The sound of it made my knees weak with want and my breath catch in my throat. I had to hang on to the wall to stop myself from running past my brother and into the arms of the man on my porch. He was *here*. I hadn't thought I'd ever hear his voice again, but apparently, I'd been wrong.

But he'd been wrong first, and he couldn't just show up and expect…whatever he was expecting.

With a deep breath and a quick reminder to keep my

clothes on this time, I pushed off the wall and padded the rest of the way down the hall. My heart beat faster the closer I came to that rectangle of light. So close, right there. He came back.

I leaned around the corner and peeked over my brother's shoulder, confirming what I had known the second I'd heard the first stuttered greeting.

Abraham Rebel Lynch stood on my front porch.

"Uh, Char?" Julian sounded uneasy, not that I blamed him. Men didn't come to the house looking for me. Plus anything new to Julian tended to make him a bit anxious these days.

"It's okay, bud." I patted his shoulder and reached around him to open the screen door the rest of the way. "Head on out before you miss the bus."

He paused for a moment, staring blankly at the man in front of him. Rebel didn't move, didn't look away from Julian's face. He waited, watching, both men standing firm in their standoff.

I very nearly rolled my eyes. "Go, Julian."

Before my brother moved, before he left me alone with the man on the porch, he pulled his shoulders back and lifted his chin. "Text me if you need me."

I grinned, ducking my head as the younger boy walked carefully out the door. Rebel slid out of his way, whispering a respectful "thank you" as Julian passed. The handsome wolfman even turned to watch my brother amble down the stairs and along the front walkway before he finally spoke.

"He's a brave one." Rebel turned his ice-blue eyes on me, making my heart stutter. "Most humans are more nervous the first time they meet one of us."

I shrugged, forcing myself to play it cool. "We don't scare easily."

He nodded once. "Noted."

I leaned a shoulder against the doorframe and crossed my

arms over my chest. The picture of nonchalance. Of course, inside was a different story—my pounding heart, the roar in my ears, the way my stomach knotted at the nearness of him. I was in a full-on fake-it-'til-you-make-it situation, not exactly what I'd had planned for seven in the morning on a random Tuesday. While wearing penguin pajamas.

"So, how can I help you, Rebel?"

He shifted his weight and ran a hand through his hair, a touching show of nervousness in an otherwise imposing figure. He looked good, which pissed me off. I'd spent the past few months alternately throwing things and sobbing into my pillows. My hair needed cutting, my skin was sallow, and the bags under my eyes had luggage of their own. Meanwhile, Rebel looked as if he'd just stepped out of a photo shoot. The bastard.

"Well, I was kind of hoping I could try to fix what we had between us." His voice was quiet, his words soft. But I'd heard that tone before from men who'd made promises they couldn't keep.

"Try to fix what, exactly?" I purposely looked him up and down, pausing at the fly of his jeans. "Because all we really had was sex. And I'm pretty sure we got that down pat from the get-go."

He huffed and shot me an irritated glare. "That's not what I meant."

"Then, please. Explain." I held my breath and waited him out. I didn't want to believe him, didn't want to get my hopes up. But he looked so nervous, and he'd made the effort to track me down. Maybe, just maybe, he was ready to apologize for being a dumbass. I still craved him, still felt the pull to him. I just wanted him not to be so stupid when it came to what a relationship needed. I wanted to know we would be in something together—not be me against him and his wolf.

Rebel took a deep breath, steeling himself it seemed. "I'd

like to begin anew."

"Anew?"

"Yes."

"As in a new what? A new start, a new life, a new mate? Where do you want to begin?"

Oh, yeah, he was getting frustrated with me. But then his lips quirked, and a small smile bloomed on his handsome face. A look that said I was in trouble. Serious, deep trouble.

"Hello. My name is Abraham Lynch, though my friends call me Rebel. I'm new in town, just moved in a few houses over, and I was wondering if you'd like to join me for a cup of coffee at the diner down the road."

My heart skittered in my chest as my entire body seemed to tingle with both excitement and something a little…dirtier. Oh lord, he'd come back for me. Like a fairy-tale princess, my prince had returned. Hopefully smarter and more willing to compromise than before.

But there'd been a poster in the hall at my high school, one that was meant to motivate and inspire. The picture had been soothing, the words white and bold. I could never remember the exact phrase or who it was accredited to, but I remembered the gist. *Showing up is not all of life, but it counts for a lot of it.*

He'd shown up.

It was my turn. "You want…coffee?"

He frowned for a second, looking unsure again. "Um, yes?"

"That's it? Just coffee?" I cocked my head and smiled. Giving him the first signal that I wasn't going to kick his hot ass off my porch. Giving him permission to try harder.

And he took that permission and ran with it. Rebel inched closer, pinning me against the doorjamb and giving me the full force of his growl.

"Just coffee? No, Charlotte. It's a start, but you should know that I want everything. I want you in my life, my bed, on my bike, and wrapped in my arms. I want to tease you and make you squirm. I want you to ride my cock until you scream, and then I want to roll you under me and make you come for hours. I want to taste you, tongue you, and fuck you until we're both too exhausted to speak." His hand shook as he raised it to run a knuckle softly down my cheek. "I want to mark you as my mate, knowing you fully understand what that means. I want to wrap you in my arms and tell you how much you mean to me, how much I miss you when you're not with me, and how much I love you. I want everything."

I swallowed hard, the weight of his words bearing down on the walls I'd erected in his absence. His speech was lovely and sweet, and I wanted to believe him. I truly did. But they were the words of a man. A man who was not always the one in control.

"You mean your wolf loves me."

"Yes, he does." Rebel refused to let me look away when I tried, pressing a finger to my chin and forcing my head up in a gentle but demanding way. "But the wolf isn't separate from the man, Charlotte. My wolf loves you because I love you, and I hope one day you'll feel the same for me. I understand your concerns and your desire to care for your family, and I'm not asking you to give anything up. I'm here, ready to take things at your speed and on your terms. I want to get to know you. Take my time to learn about you, build a friendship with you, and fall in love with you. As a man, not just as a wolf. You're my soul mate. I want a chance to show you what that means."

I swallowed hard, the need to touch him, to surrender, growing. The sting of tears building. "And your bike? Your club?"

"I'm on hiatus. I haven't left the club, but I've stored my cut in the closet and all my bikes in the garage. For now." He shrugged at what had to be my most surprised face ever. "When you decide if I'm worthy enough to share your life with, then we can discuss the future of my bike and my club. Together."

Hope flared bright and hot in my chest. "No demanding?"

He shook his head slowly, keeping his eyes on mine. Staying honest. "No demanding. We go at your pace."

My grin had to be huge. He'd handed me the golden ticket. Everything I could have wanted or needed from him, he offered. We still had a lot to learn and discover about each other, but he'd just given us the time we needed. The time I'd originally asked for. We'd work on our friendship, on our relationship. We'd give both plenty of time to grow strong and true. But the third part of our relationship? The lust part? Yeah. That was hot, bright, and about to explode.

Ready to show him exactly what pace I wanted, I ran my fingers over the waistband of his jeans. Pulling him closer. "And if my pace is a little faster than yours?"

His eyes darkened, and his lips turned up in a smile. "Whatever you want, kitten."

Exactly what I wanted to hear. I grabbed his shirt and pulled him against me, rubbing my nose along his jaw. I'd missed his scent. Missed the way his presence made my body throb with need for him. I'd missed every inch of him. One night with this man was all it had taken to become addicted, and I was beyond ready for my next fix.

"And if I said I wanted you to throw me down and make me scream your name?"

His hands slid up my legs to grip my waist, twisting me until his erection nudged my hip.

"I would be obliged to follow your direction."

His lips were millimeters from mine, his warm breath washing over my face on every exhale. I felt his want for me, knew that level of desire as it matched my own. He'd come to me with the exact promises I needed to hear. Who knew how it would work out or if we'd be able to figure out our differences, but the fact that he'd shown up, that he'd made concessions and offered promises, was enough. For now.

"Hey, Abraham?" I pressed my hips into his, rubbing against his dick and earning a low growl.

"Yes, Charlotte?" His hands massaged my ass, kneading the flesh roughly as his lips found their way to my neck.

"I think I'd like that coffee now."

He stopped groping me, pulling back to look me in the eye. "Now?"

I nodded and smiled. "Yes, now. Though we don't have to go out, you know. I have a lovely coffeepot right inside."

He flicked his gaze behind me, almost imperceptible in its speed. "Inside there?"

I nodded and hooked my fingers into the belt loops of his jeans. His expression went from confusion to wicked smirk in less than a second. Oh yeah, he knew what I wanted. Which was good, because I doubted I could last another minute without him touching at least some part of me. Maybe all the parts of me.

Needing more—and not wanting to get arrested for taking it—I tugged Rebel with me as I stepped into the house. But the man never could give up all of his control. He paused in the doorway, his arms up and his hands braced against the doorjamb as he leaned into the hall.

"So what you're saying is you want me inside?" The glint in his eyes told me he knew exactly what he'd done with the double entendre. I pulled harder, but he resisted, lifting a single eyebrow as he waited for my answer.

I finally huffed. "Yes. I want you inside."

He took one step into the hall. "And we'll have coffee."

Joke...over. I pulled him against me, pushing my chest

flush with his. My nipples were hard, my panties were wet, and I was tired of the teasing game we were playing. It was time to give in.

"If by 'have coffee' you mean have hot makeup sex on every available flat surface in this house, then yes. We will have lots and lots of coffee. Coffee in every room. Coffee at all hours so long as my brother isn't home. There will be a coffee bonanza, just get your ass in here."

He picked me up and kicked the door closed, his lips meeting mine in a brutal kiss. My body shuddered, relief and desire dancing through me as he tangled his tongue with mine. I wrapped my arms and legs around him, clinging to him with everything I had, as he strode through my little house. We kissed with the aggression born from being apart too long, teeth knocking and tongues stroking until finally I pulled away to catch my breath. Rebel took that moment to grin and ease me back on the kitchen table.

This has some serious promise.

With a quick yank, he removed my pajama pants and the panties underneath, leaving me bare on the bottom half. Exposed. I was so, so wet for him. So needy. With every breath on my thigh, I moaned. Every brush of his fingers over me, I sighed. This was what I'd needed. Him. Us.

Always.

With a sweet, soft kiss to my breast, Rebel dropped to his knees and pulled my calves over his shoulders, spreading me before him. Shooting me that trademark little grin as he pressed his thumb to my clit and began a wicked, slow grind.

"Hey, Charlotte?"

My legs shook as he slid two fingers inside. "Yeah?"

"I think I'm going to fucking love coffee."

My back arched off the table as his tongue met my flesh, and my hands fisted into his hair. Yes, this was what I'd been missing. What I'd needed. What only Rebel could give me.

The feeling of utter and total surrender.

"Me too, Reb. Me too."

He waited four hundred years for her.

She only ever wanted to find her mate.

Their time has come.

CLAIMING HIS NEED

FERAL BREED MOTORCYCLE CLUB
BOOK TWO

AVAILABLE NOW

ACKNOWLEDGMENTS

To all my friends from my fandom life, thank you. Without the women I've met over these last too-many years, I never would have had the guts and the will to hit the publish button.

To my soul mate, Heather, for her unwavering support, even in the face of a sub-genre she wouldn't normally read.

To Esher, for taking her first steps into the paranormal realm with this novella and offering me words of wisdom and support.

To Felicia, for reading my story and making sure I didn't commit some kind of naughty-word faux pas.

To Lisa, for making sure I figured out when to use into and in to and for spreading the good word on the difference between rein and reign. *How you likin' the reign, girl?*

To Caren, for always being there when I need a proofreader, a touchstone, a voice of reason, or just someone to send ranty text messages to.

To Brighton, who taught me a lot along the way and continues to share her knowledge with those of us coming up the ladder behind her.

Oh, and to my husband. I have no idea how he puts up with me.

ACKNOWLEDGMENTS

This section could go on for pages and pages, but I won't torture anyone with that. Just know that if at any time you tweeted me, liked my page, sent me a review, a message, an email, a picture, told me how to Facebook stalk your cowboy kind-of-cousin for research, met me for coffee, met me for not-coffee, encouraged my funnel cake obsession, or clicked on one of the stories I posted along the way and lurked your way through it, this is me saying thank you.

Edited by Silently Correcting Your Grammar, LLC
Cover Art by Cormar Covers

ABOUT THE AUTHOR

A storyteller from the time she could talk, *USA Today* bestselling author Ellis grew up among family legends of hauntings, psychics, and love spanning decades. Those stories didn't always have the happiest of endings, so they inspired her to write about real life, real love, and the difficulties therein. From farmers to werewolves, store clerks to witches—if there's love to be found, she'll write about it. Ellis lives in the Chicago area with her husband, daughters, and two tiny fish that take up way too much of her time.

Find Ellis online at:
Website: www.ellisleigh.com
Twitter: https://twitter.com/ellis_writes
Facebook: https://www.facebook.com/ellisleighwrites
Newsletter sign up: http://www.ellisleigh.com/newsletter